A GIRL CALLED DEBBIE

There's more to Nurse Debbie Holden than meets the eye: she has cared for Dermot Gregory's lonely little boy, restored his sick mother to health and stolen into her employer's heart whilst she's helped on his farm. Debbie has also impressed professional dancer Michael Thornton with her dancing skills, prompting him to offer her a new career and a proposal of marriage . . . But what is Debbie's secret? Is it too late for Dermot to discover?

ELIZABETH BRENNAN

A GIRL CALLED DEBBIE

Complete and Unabridged

LINFORD
Leicester

First published in Great Britain in 1975 by
Robert Hale & Company
London

First Linford Edition
published 2008
by arrangement with
Robert Hale Limited
London

British Library CIP Data

Brennan, Elizabeth
A girl called Debbie.—Large print ed.—
Linford romance library
1. Nurses—Fiction 2. Love stories
3. Large type books
I. Title
823.9'14 [F]

ISBN 978–1–84782–484–4

Published by
F. A. Thorpe (Publishing)
Anstey, Leicestershire

Set by Words & Graphics Ltd.
Anstey, Leicestershire
Printed and bound in Great Britain by
T. J. International Ltd., Padstow, Cornwall

'For Mark, Michael and Johnnie!
Best boys at St. Gerards.'

1

Coming up the drive, holding Mark's small hand as they walked, Debbie Holden glimpsed a quick view of her employer's blue polo-necked pullover as he crossed the gravelled area in front of the Old Abbey Farm House. He was obviously in a hurry walking quickly round to the back, where the stables and the farmyards, half hidden by trees, merged away down towards the river.

'There's Daddy, Mark.'

'I see Daddy! I see him — ' The five-year-old boy snatched away his hand, and sped as fast as his small legs could carry him, holding tightly to a bunch of snowdrops, in the wake of his vanishing parent.

Debbie slowed down. It was no use. She'd never catch the little bit of quick-silver that was Mark. Let him run and find his father. She lifted her eyes to the grey mountains surrounding the farm, their jagged outlines half hidden by mist, their crests snow-covered, with a sigh. These rugged hills, this homely farm, the child, the Gregorys — were all becoming far too dear to her. The bleak greyness of the February evening was getting even colder, but still, she told herself, the days were getting longer, and snowdrops gleamed whitely along the banks and in mossy corners under the bare trees.

She could hear men's voices across the yard, and then Dermot Gregory emerged from a shed in which his prize bull was being visited by a neighbouring farmer, and his one cow-man was holding forth on the beast's chances at the next agricultural show.

'Hallo, Deb!' Dermot came across to her, carrying Mark on his shoulder. 'This fellow seems the better for his outing.'

'He loved it in spite of the cold. You got your flowers, of course?' she queried, smiling. 'He picked them himself for you! Clutched them so tightly all the way home I'm afraid the poor things are strangled!'

'They'll revive!' Dermot lifted the child down.

'We all do!' Debbie observed, then wondered what made her pass that remark, and coloured.

The young farmer glanced at her curiously for a moment, out of disillusioned grey eyes. He was a tall man with very square shoulders, though he was almost painfully thin, and with rather harsh features, softened a little sometimes when he was less unhappy, as now. His dark hair was tumbled, after Mark's handling, imparting a more youthful aspect than normally. 'I suppose we do,' he agreed, after a moment's hesitation. 'I suppose in the nature of things, we do.'

'Come along then, Scallywag! It's time for tea.' She made an effort to catch Mark's hand.

'But I want to see the big bull again, an' I want to give the horse a sugar-lump — you promised.' He was off to the sheds again, and Debbie had to follow him, running between the talking men.

'Now then,' his father called out, 'back here, young fellow. You've seen the bull, and you can visit Big Boy, tomorrow. We didn't promise that for today. That's tomorrow. Come along.'

With a martyr-like expression on his quite extraordinarily lovely little face, Mark dragged his stout shoes over the yard back to Debbie, resigned to go indoors, where Mrs. Gregory, Dermot's mother, was preparing tea, in the big, modernised country kitchen.

Mrs. Gregory was a frail woman, young looking for her years, but since her illness having often a worried aspect, despite her ready, very attractive smile. As the girl looked at her ex-patient now, she could not but own the vast and continuing improvement in the woman's health. Though she had once wanted to die, Dermot's mother was going to make a complete recovery.

It would take time, still, but she would get well.

'You shouldn't have bothered getting tea, Mrs. Gregory. But I suppose you had despaired of getting any, today! You see, we had to stop every now and then to pick snowdrops! And I forgot all about it being Mrs. Ramsay's day off.'

'They're for Daddy, Nana. Can I put them in water?' Mark grabbed his mug from the table.

'Yes, but *not* in your tea-mug!' Debbie hurried the child out of his coat and woolly gloves and found a glass holder, while the older woman poured out tea and took a plate of hot, buttered scones from the top of the Aga.

'I can't resist Mrs. Ramsay's scones!' she admitted ruefully. 'They're delicious — even if they're supposed to be bad for me!'

'I don't think one or two will do you any harm! Sit down and enjoy them straight away. I'll see to this young man.'

'Bless you! But do come and join me.

It's so cold, and you must be longing for a 'cuppa'.'

'Snow on the hills, still! But see how the daylight lingers!'

'What an optimist you are, Debbie! I don't think I've ever heard you being gloomy. You are so good for me — for us all!' laughed Mrs. Gregory.

The two chatted, relaxed, 'at home' in each other's company.

'It's my birthday tomorrow, Nana,' Mark managed to interrupt, between mouthfuls of scone and tea. 'I'll be five! Hurrah — I'll be five! And I'm going to get heaps of presents!'

'Indeed!' Debbie grinned, 'and don't stuff!'

'Strange,' Mrs. Gregory's voice trembled a little, 'I was thinking before you came in just now, you have been five whole years with us, Deb dear! Sometimes I try to think of when you were *not* here, and I really can't manage it! We seem to have known and — loved — you, always.'

'Well, I feel the same way, too,' her companion declared, briskly, quelling the threat of emotion in their reminiscing. 'It's — well,' she laughed, 'let's say, it's home, now, for me really and truly HOME.'

'I'm so glad. I hope you will always feel that way.' Mrs. Gregory paused. 'Poor darling Ann — will Dermot ever get over it? One precious year of such happy marriage — and then to lose her, and his little son — only for you, my dear, only for you, the child couldn't have survived.'

'What a blessing I happened to be available.' The brown-eyed girl glanced at the busily occupied Mark, with a look of adoration. 'And yes, Dermot is getting over it. Do remember, too, Mrs. Gregory, Ann would have been a cripple — absolutely helpless. Who'd want that? She certainly would not.'

'None of us would. It's only the reminders — the time of year, snow on the hills — Mark's fifth birthday — this very day — no, tomorrow, five years ago.'

'I do understand.' Debbie laid a

quick, square hand over her friend's slender, not quite steady one. They were friends now, Nurse Deborah Holden and her one-time patient.

'I so often wonder what possessed her, to go off on that horse within a few days of her child's birth? A sudden whim to be up and doing, I suppose, poor girl.'

'No use speculating over all that now, Mrs. Gregory. It seems Ann valued that particular horse above all the others, for the very reason we now deplore — his spirit, his unpredictability — even his 'gaiety', if an animal could ever be said to possess such a quality. The horse and the rider matched each other. Probably only meant to canter quietly round the paddocks. When the accident happened she can have known nothing about it — so glad I happened to be within call.'

'Yes, indeed, and how strange that you were to have gone back to the hospital in London that day, only you missed your train?'

Debbie looked thoughtful, half-smiling, half serious. 'Destiny, I suppose? Providence? Everything ready, my case packed. I thought your phone call was, in fact, my taxi-man! Matron understood, of course. But I had been telling her some time previously that I would like to do private nursing for a while.'

'So things worked out marvellously, for us, I mean!'

'For me, too! It was all 'for luck' — my missing that train.'

Mrs. Gregory helped herself to another cup of tea. Obviously she wanted to talk, and it was good for her to be able to talk. Shut up within herself she had been for so long, mentally as well as physically ill. It was an excellent sign that she could now, at last, talk about the tragedy of the past few years — her late husband's excesses in drinking, the way he had neglected the farm and mortgaged acre after acre of good inherited land, until bankruptcy seemed inevitable. Then, on the very eve of Dermot's marriage to Ann, his father had been killed in a drunken car accident. Despite her life of almost despairing unhappiness, Mrs. Gregory had mourned her unfortunate, 'good-for-nothing' husband. The shock of his sudden death, on top of years of accumulated money troubles, had stricken her into serious illness, necessitating months in hospital, and the home-coming to which she had been so looking forward, to Dermot and his young wife, had been a coming back to fresh, even more poignant tragedy.

Desperate with grief, Dermot had dismissed the well-meant but reluctant offers from relations, knowing that such suggested arrangements could never have worked, either for them, or for him. He had gone to the nursery, prepared so lovingly by Ann, for her baby, and had begged Nurse Holden to remain on at the farm, not only as 'Nanny' or 'foster-mother' to his infant son, but to nurse his mother, who at that time 'wanted to die'. Wages, far exceeding any hitherto earned by the girl, were offered, and a spacious bed-sitter of her own, with every facility for a comfortable life, if she would but stay long enough to get the little newcomer 'on his feet', and Mrs. Gregory sufficiently restored to face life, again.

Debbie had not dreamed of remaining. She had been fully resolved on another year at the hospital in London. But something in Dermot's haunted grey eyes, that evening, when he had come in such grief and trouble to the nursery, had touched the generous heart of the brisk, sensible young nurse. She agreed to stay.

That was five years ago, five years filled with a deepening sense of achievement and satisfaction in her work, such as she had never known before. Debbie grew to love little Mark as his own mother would have done, and in fact, in every respect, became a mother to the child, who in turn, found in her all that a child could find in the most tender parent. Gratitude and regard from both Mrs. Gregory and Dermot deepened into friendship, until 'Nurse Holden' became simply 'Debbie', one of the family, sharing in all their concerns. The Old Abbey Farm was, indeed, home, for she had no other real home, both her parents being recently dead, and her older sister married, with two children, living in a bungalow outside Rockinish, the market town, three miles away from the farm. Debbie had been invited to make her home with her sister, but except for visits, or week-end holidays, much as she liked her sister and brother-in-law, Debbie had no intention of imposing on them. Independent, even to a fault, she was determined to stand on her own feet, in life.

But, on that cold snowy February day, Debbie faced the fact that she had a problem to solve. Yet another tie, of late, was binding her to the Old Abbey Farm. She was in love with Dermot — with all the strength of a steady deeply passionate, yet as deeply reserved nature — a character born with the inherent tendency to stand, rock-like, by loyalties of heart, or of convinced principles. For her, loving was the whole of life.

Gratitude, an easy-going comradeship, an admiring friendliness, a brotherly regard — was the extent of Dermot Gregory's feelings for Debbie, not at all conscious attitudes, but nevertheless, genuine. Untested, he was not aware of the strength of them, nor of a certain taken-for-granted acceptance of her presence and her loyalty, a sort of sub-conscious supposition of her permanent availability.

2

The living room at the Old Abbey Farmhouse was a long, low-ceilinged place with exposed beams, more comfortable than elegant. A happy, lived-in atmosphere pervaded it with flowers and books, farming journals and such like, not only in their appointed shelves, but generally overflowing on to chairs and floor. After the evening meal, Dermot, in a comfortable tweed jacket and house-shoes, was accustomed to wander in there for coffee with his mother and Debbie, for the girl had long ago given up all pretence of keeping to her own bed-sitter, except to sleep there.

Sometimes there was a television programme in which everyone was interested, or discs on the record player, sometimes people dropped in, while Mrs. Gregory knitted Aran jerseys for

Mark. Always Debbie made tea later in the night before bed-time, if she were at home. Occasionally she was not at home, for she loved dancing, and had no lack of partners, either to call for her, or to dance with her. She was generally regarded as 'a nice, plain type of lassie, and a damned good dancer', by the local farmers.

When she came into the sitting room on that evening, Mark being safely in bed and Mrs. Ramsay gone to spend the night with relations, Dermot glanced up from his accounts to meet her warm smile. After a while, although she had curled up in a big chair, ostensibly to write letters, he was aware of her unblinking regard. 'A smut on my nose, or something, Deb!' he smiled.

'Er — oh, not at all! Sorry! Was I staring at you!' She returned hotly embarrassed, to her letter.

'I see you brought back your usual supply from the library,' he observed then, indicating the pile of books on the floor beside Debbie's chair. 'How you get through all those books — '

She laughed. 'I don't, really. I browse, sort of, until I discover something worth reading. Oh, and by-the-way — ' She glanced up at an impressive but very old painting, set in a panel over the fire-place, a lady on horseback. 'I dropped into the museum!'

'As usual!'

'Well, yes, I often do!'

'How's old Devlin? Still convinced we have a masterpiece here?' With the stem of his pipe he pointed to the panel. 'The only value it has for me is that horse! The Gregorys were all horse lovers! Not always to their advantage financially. A rakish lot of ancestors I've had, Ma, dear!'

His mother smiled. 'Not all of them. You exaggerate. Most of them were great farming men, to own and keep so much good land — for so long.'

'Except for their drinking habits, they were all right. So many of them were chronic alcoholics!' He stopped, non-plussed, and angry with himself. 'Sorry,

Ma. I didn't mean — '

'It's all right, my dear. I know you meant no harm.' Mrs. Gregory hastened to change the subject. 'It's the young lady I admire! I've always maintained she has a look of the Gregorys — the nose, certainly, and the shape of the head, even the mouth — ' They looked up at the oil painting, so familiar to them that it was no longer much noticed. The canvas was dimmed by age, the rich colouring obscured by dirt and smoke. A lady in a blue habit with a feather in her hat, smiled over her shoulder, riding beneath heavy summer trees. The Old Abbey, then a real Abbey, belonging to some religious order, just discernible in the distance.

'Ah, well — ' The hard look returned to Dermot's face. 'Gone are the days!'

'But don't forget you've got one fine hunter! What about Big Boy,' Debbie reminded him, laughing.

'A luxury I can't afford. Madness to keep him, under the circumstances. Haven't time or money to have him

17

trained, as he should be. He's got great stuff in him — that fellow.'

'Yes, indeed.' Debbie agreed, and then went on, 'but I was going to tell you — about Mr. Devlin — he's absolutely convinced it's a Wootton, and he is at the moment in correspondence, again, with *The Times*, about it.'

'Poor man!' Mrs. Gregory sighed. 'He's been interested in that painting most of his life — seems to be forever corresponding with someone or other about it.'

'And you've had it valued?' Debbie suggested.

'In a sort of way. Not by an expert. That's what I'm always saying to Dermot,' his mother complained.

'Not worth the trouble — and expense,' he retorted, impatiently, for the subject had been for years a recurring irritation, a little 'bone of contention' between them.

'And you were *offered* several hundreds for it, even as it is — even if it's not a Wootton. I've thought you foolish not to sell it, if only to have a horse entered with some hopes at the Lakeview Races!'

'What nonsense, Ma! Where'd be the use selling a family heirloom for a few miserable hundreds, now-a-days.'

'But can we afford an heirloom?' his mother smiled, recognising the familiar signs of irritation, and making an effort to treat the subject lightly for that reason.

'Dermot may be very wise — holding on to it,' Debbie interposed. 'Who knows!'

'Optimist!' Restored to placidity, he laughed across the leaping firelight into the brown eyes so often and so kindly turned towards him. Then he filled his pipe and resumed work on his accounts, his hair ruffled and the familiar frown of concentration returning. Despite the harshness of his face, Debbie thought, just then, how handsome this young farmer employer of hers was. Embittered, it was true, by battles with poverty, and the loss of the young wife he had so truly loved, sometimes truculent, even morose, yet how charming, even boyishly genial he could sometimes be.

A china clock ticked on the mantelpiece. The firelogs hissed and blazed. Sometimes hailstones lashed the curtained windows outside. Gusts of wind roared round the old house. Debbie saw that Mrs. Gregory was happily engaged on an intricate knitting pattern, and she returned to the letter which she was writing to her sister, contented. If things could remain forever like this, she suddenly thought, nibbling the end of her Biro, and staring into the fire, she'd be happy enough here with Dermot and his mother in this firelit, lovely intimacy. She'd be content, despite the urges and demands of her heart for so much more, to go on loving this man, even if he never knew it — could the wheel of Time stop here, at this degree of quiet togetherness.

But Time never stands still, and into

the peace of the room, the telephone shrilled in the hall.

'I'll take it.' She hurried out of her chair.

'Thanks.' murmured Dermot, deep in form filling.

In about five minutes' time Debbie returned, her face alight with the import of news. 'I say — that's Mr. Devlin, of all people! He'd like to speak to you, Dermot.'

A trifle impatiently the young man rose and left the room.

Debbie waltzed about the room. 'Oh, Mrs. Gregory — don't think I'm mad!' She came to rest on the hearth rug. 'Talk of angels! With spectacles half way down their noses! That's the way he wears them, bless him! Talk about heirlooms and paintings! I do believe he's on to something, at last!'

The older woman dropped her work in amazement. 'How, my dear? What had he to say? Whatever it is — if he thinks it's good — it will probably turn out to be too good to be true!'

'Not this time. At least — oh, there's a real hope now! He says there's an article in *The Times* — where's yesterday's *Times*?' She started to hunt about the room, in a whirl of impatience.

'Goodness — I don't think any of us had time even to look at it yesterday. I meant to, after lunch, but forgot when those wretched income tax people arrived. And I'm sure Dermot hadn't a moment to spare, and was intending to glance at the leading article before going to bed, as usual.'

'I have it! Under the settee cushions!' Debbie snatched the newspaper, quickly opening it out on the settee. 'It's never been opened!'

She had just commenced flicking through the pages when Dermot came back into the room. 'Come on — tell us! she laughed. 'We can't wait! I've found the paper, but — '

'Nothing proved, whatsoever,' the young man observed, soberly, as she handed him *The Times*. 'That old canvas there is probably a copy like all the rest. I hear there are at least three of them floating around. Ah — here we are! Now, Ma, it's all yours!' He pulled forward her small table to spread out the page before her, not heeding the scattered needles and knitting. 'Yours the privilege of looking at it, first!'

There, rather prominently displayed, was a sizeable picture of their canvas, looking quite striking in black and white, and heading it, in large print — 'The missing Wootton? New York Dealer's search.' Underneath, was a short article by a representative of a firm of London Art and Antique Dealers and Auctioneers. Gerald Van St. Ledger, wealthy collector, was searching for the 'Lady on Horseback', which was thought to be still in existence somewhere in England, but more probably in Ireland. A fortune awaited the unknown owner.

Mrs. Gregory looked up with excited colour in her faded face. 'Your father — poor Tom — always claimed it was an original! Lots of people told him it was probably valuable. But he was, like you, Dermot, hard to convince. Well, well — perhaps now the luck of the Gregorys is at last turning!' she concluded, with tears, wiping her glasses.

'I say — that must have been what Colonel Penrose meant when he met me in the High Street this morning,' Debbie exclaimed, turning to Dermot, who was again searching the margin of the painting in a vain effort to distinguish the initials.

'Even the initials — couldn't they be copied, too! But you can't see the damn thing any more with dirt! No one could ever make out the initials, anyway.'

'But what did the colonel say?' Mrs. Gregory wanted to know. 'I'm so glad he is back again living in Penrose House — and with his daughter. I hear she is a widow, poor girl — so young, too. They intend settling in their old house in Rockinish, to start a riding school. But what did the Colonel say?'

'Why he just called out a greeting across the street, you know his way! Then he laughed and said something about a fortune coming our way.' I thought he was joking, though I couldn't see the point! Would he remember seeing the picture, Mrs. Gregory?'

'Of course, he would. Indeed, I remember his admiring it, once. He was here a few times on business with poor Tom.'

Dermot turned away from the panel. 'Ah — that explains it!' he smiled a little grimly. 'That's it!'

'I don't understand? You have such an awkward way of saying things, as though we could read your thoughts!' his mother complained testily.

'Sorry, Ma! I simply mean that this explains Meriel's dulcet tones on the phone this morning. She had a phone beside her bed it seems, and when she saw *The Times*, I suppose she thought it might be worth getting in touch with us. We might soon even be sociably acceptable — even worth cultivating.

Yes — she explained that she had a phone beside her bed!' he grinned.

'I think you are horrid, Dermot. They're such nice people. It would be so pleasant for me to be on terms with them. I'm told Meriel's husband died only recently — that's why they came home. He seems to have been a well-to-do man, but I hear he left her nothing.'

'Well — if you want to get on terms with them, you can cheer up, Ma, dear! She said her dad was intending to call on us, and that she'd give herself that pleasure, too. So our social position is assured!'

'Don't be so absurd!' Debbie chided, laughing. 'You sound so cynical at times. And it annoys your mother. Don't heed him, darling!' She bent to tidy back the wool and knitting needles. 'Now I'll go and make us all some tea as usual, and that will calm us down! Then — perhaps — Mrs. Gregory, you and Dermot might like to talk business, So I'll take a book and be off to my room.'

'You'll do no such thing!' her friend exclaimed. 'Bring the tea, my love, and stay right here with us. Only for you, indeed, we would probably be a long time without knowledge of all this. After all, you kept on dropping in on old Mr. Devlin, and believing in him. You certainly got no encouragement here!' she concluded with a dark glance at her son, which he completely disregarded.

'Stay and advise us!' Dermot smiled. 'Indeed, Deb — it's a bit late in the day for you to opt out on our business sessions! Don't be silly!'

'That's all right, then,' she laughed. 'Back in a few moments with the tea.'

'I wonder if Meriel is still as beautiful as she was when they left Penrose House! And if she's still as hard as nails, and a jealous cat! I shall never forget her treatment of Ann,' Dermot mused grimly. 'Lucky for them they were able to get rid of their tenant.'

'Anyway, it was nice of her to ring. And I hope they will call.' Mrs.

Gregory hesitated. 'I'd like to meet people again, socially. One gets so weary of being an invalid and cut off from everybody.'

Dermot bent and kissed the top of her head. 'Not to worry, Ma! When people know you're able to be up and about, again, you'll have more of them than you'll want. Even Meriel — beautiful, dashing creature! She's bound to call — like a blonde bombshell!'

At that moment, Debbie had just entered the room, and so overheard Dermot's final remarks regarding the colonel's daughter. The lightly spoken words made little impression on her at the time, but later, she remembered them. Tea was very welcome. Talk was continuous and excited, but mostly between the two women, for Dermot paced the floor, cup in hand, for the most part in silence.

'So our first step, immediately, will be to have the painting valued by an acknowledged expert?' his mother inquired.

'I suppose so.' He sat down restlessly.

'But that will cost us a nice penny! Probably a hair-brained scheme.'

'Oh, but, surely — ' Debbie began.

'I just dislike the idea of making a fool of myself! After all the fuss and expense it's quite likely that old panel is only a copy, like the others mentioned in *The Times*.'

'You *are* an old pessimist!' Debbie accused, really annoyed at the effect of his remark on his mother.

'Maybe! But we have to be realistic.' He crossed one long leg over the other, gloomily.

'But,' Mrs. Gregory insisted, 'why always imagine the worst? Why not be hopeful!'

'Because, dear mother, the worst so damned often happens.'

'Look at it this way — that canvas has been in your family for — goodness — must be generations. This house is three hundred years old, parts of it older, your father used to say, and your grandfather claimed he remembered it being in a huge gilt frame, one time, and that lady is supposed to be an ancestor. I insist she has a look of the Gregorys, too!'

'Can't say I've noticed it.'

Debbie emptied the last of the contents of the teapot into her cup. 'Your mother has been outlining all you could do, Dermot — while you've been pacing the floor, your thoughts a hundred leagues away! I don't believe you heard a word!'

'Well — what shall we do with this mythical fortune, Deb? You must tell us. Sensible girl — head well screwed on! Feet on the ground — when not dancing, of course!'

'For two pins I wouldn't tell you,' she laughed. 'I wish you wouldn't laugh at us.' She blushed under his amused gaze. 'Anyhow it's no harm to dream!'

'No, it's no harm to dream,' he agreed. 'Trouble is you don't, as a rule, know you're dreaming when you are at it! But, go ahead — what shall we do with those thousands when our ship comes in, and our ancient painting, minus even its gilt frame, goes out?'

'First — pay back the debt? That's what your mother most wants.' She paused, 'Then buy back the Long Acre fields beyond Knockadee!'

'At about ten times the price we sold them for, five or six years ago!'

There was a defiantly optimistic smile in the girl's expressive large brown eyes. Dermot thought he had never seen those liquid orbs so full of light and happiness, the whites so clear and blue-tinted, the ridiculous lashes seeming to curl up, star-like. He thought, suddenly, what a terribly nice sort of girl she was, and how fond he was of her — what a friend she had been. And now at the bare idea of his own and his mother's prosperity, her happiness was so evident. How wise and down-to-earth she was too about those Long Acre fields — exactly his own most secret hope and ambition. 'If you did nothing else, that must be first,' she amended seriously.

Mrs. Gregory interposed, enthusiastically, 'And new farm machinery — the yards and out-houses modernised!'

'Sure! Sure! Everything modernised! And new stock, eh? And a couple of good men?'

The three laughed. Suddenly, they were all happy. Whether all this hope were the wildest nonsense, or an extraordinary bit of luck — they were all happy, just then, thinking about it, talking and laughing about it.

'Oh, yes, and Big Boy trained to run at all the point-to-points, and carry home the cup at the Lakeview Races!' Debbie exclaimed throwing a cushion on the floor in her exuberance. Then she picked it up, tidied her letter writing materials, and collected the teacups. 'Oh, well — it's been fun!' She waited at the door a moment in silence. 'But, seriously, I believe, this time LUCK is coming our way! Do say you at least have a hope, Dermot?'

He jumped up and took the tray from her. 'I'll take those into the kitchen. I'm going in there. Sorry to have been so damping. Even if I can't help feeling sceptical, I've no right to spread gloom. I'll take these out.' He stood with the tray in his hands by the door. 'Seriously, I'll get in touch with O'Connor first thing in the morning. A solicitor on the job, is, I take it, the first essential? A necessary risk, I suppose, eh, Ma, dear?'

'Yes, to be sure, Dermot. And risks are part of life. No one ever achieved anything without taking some sort of risk!'

'I'll do that, then. And he can arrange for an expert valuer's opinion. Meanwhile he can write to *The Times* for us.'

'Now you're talking sense!' Debbie declared.

'May as well be hung for a sheep as a lamb!' he grinned. 'Solicitors, valuers, what-have-you! But you have to spend money in order to make money? Isn't that your theory, Debbie?'

'It certainly would be — if I were in a position to try it out!' she laughingly conceded.

Dermot left with the tray and his account books. In a few minutes he went into his office, closing the door, where Debbie knew he would work long after everyone else had gone to bed. She felt, suddenly a little weary and deflated. There was something at the back of her mind she had to question, some niggling cloud over the evening's happiness. In response to a growing sense of curiosity, she inquired, 'Miss Penrose — that's not her name now, I know, but this Meriel — I overheard Dermot saying she was very beautiful?'

Mrs. Gregory looked up from a second reading of the *Times* article. 'Oh, yes, to be sure she was. Poor young thing, and I've forgotten her married name, though I did hear it Some wealthy man in England, but I believe he left her nothing — that's why she's starting this Riding School. The Colonel has some fortune — he'll help her.'

'Is it true — she didn't like Ann? I gathered from what Dermot said tonight — ?'

'At one time she was very fond of Dermot, and jealous of poor Ann. She showed it, most regrettably, but she was young, you know, then, so we don't think any more about it, especially now she's come back to start life over again. Wouldn't you agree, dear?'

'Indeed, I do agree. Well — I think I'll be off to bed,' Debbie yawned. 'It's been such an exciting evening, hasn't it! Goodnight darling. Sleep well.'

Debbie climbed very slowly upstairs. A new happiness and a strange new dread mingled in her thoughts. Meriel, very beautiful, now a young attractive widow, once in love with Dermot, come back home to live and work three miles away in Rockinish, and taking the trouble to phone Dermot from her bedside phone. Was there something significant about such a phone call?

It was as though a heavy stone had dropped into the limpid pool of life at the Old Abbey Farm house, and already, the ripples seemed to be spreading —

3

But Dermot Gregory was mistaken when he supposed that Meriel Dean (née Penrose) got in touch with him by phone that morning out of newly awakened curiosity regarding his picture. She would be the first to rejoice in any hint of new prosperity for the Gregorys, it is true. But Meriel's object in contacting Dermot, after some five years, was simply that she had made up her mind to marry him.

In a fit of pique she had married Oscar Dean, a man of seemingly considerable wealth, but old enough to be her father — indeed, he was, in fact, a year or so older than the colonel. She had been able to persuade her father, much against his will, to leave their old home in the High Street of the Irish country town where she had been born, and Oscar had backed up her persuasions by offering Colonel Penrose a spacious flat in Chelsea, at a nominal rent. Obsessed by his passion for the young and lovely blonde, and determined to keep her with him to share in the fashionable world in which he lived, he wanted no escape route for Meriel's possible return to Ireland.

It had, however, taken all her own and her new husband's powers of persuasion to move her father from that friendly, cheerful place, and the fine old house he loved, despite its crying need of repairs, for although he had enough financial security to be free of any real worry, there was little enough actual capital, nor the means of keeping up such an enormous house in the way his fathers had been accustomed to keeping it. The colonel's tastes were simple. He enjoyed living among the ordinary folk of the town. He was a keen sportsman, and there was plenty of rough shooting in that wild, mountainous district. Everybody knew him, and everybody looked up to 'the Penroses' in Rockinish. This was all a nice, comfortable sort of feeling that grew on a man, so that he took it for granted, until the threat of having to leave it came along. In London, he had mused, unhappily, nobody but strangers — the Deans, and such like — and a few of his own stiff, distant relations, would know him! It would be a frightful uprooting. Nevertheless, he did it, for Meriel, for his one child had always been the 'apple of his eye', and the real love of his life. He guessed something of her disappointment with regard to 'young Gregory', and he also guessed rightly, that beyond the enjoyment of her husband's social position, she would have little of any other kind of happiness in her marriage. He had, indeed, endeavoured to prevent the marriage, but Meriel had made up her mind that if she could not have the man she loved, she would have a rich adoring husband, race horses, a beautiful car, social prestige and a mink coat. Most of these she had achieved after marrying Oscar, his gratitude to her for allowing him to love her being such that he could refuse her nothing. It was only long afterwards that Meriel realised how much effort it had cost Oscar to give some of these requirements.

So Penrose House had been let, and Meriel's father had settled into the flat in Chelsea, secretly a most unhappy man. He had insisted, however, on a compromise. He would live in London to please Meriel, but would only let his house at home for five years, the lease to be, or not to be renewed, as the colonel would then decide.

A year before the lease ran out, his son-in-law had been killed in an air crash, leaving Meriel, after two years of marriage, unprovided for, because 'poor Oscar's' supposed fortune was by then non-existent. His craze for buying and selling horses and speculating in a large way in the bloodstock market had made such inroads into his Dean inheritance that there was little enough left by the time he met Meriel.

Some magnificent horses Oscar Dean

still possessed, and as a man about town with the wealthy Dean family behind him, there was, as yet, little to show that his circumstances had been radically changed. Everyone believed him to be still a rich man.

Meriel believed this, too, and was not undeceived until his death, when she found herself as bereft of fortune as she had been when she and Oscar had first met.

'Back to square one', was how Meriel mentally regarded herself, after the funeral. But she was thankful that 'dear old Oscar' had not lived long enough to realise how little she cared for him. She had not admitted, even to her father, how hollow her marriage had proved to be, nor how difficult it was becoming to act the part she was expected to play. In the fashionable social whirl in which she had lived for two short years there should have been little time for regrets, or for brooding. Yet regrets intruded, and the memory of Dermot Gregory had never quite faded from her mind.

They had parted on the worst possible terms, for she had not been able to hide her dislike and jealousy of Ann.

Despite this, Meriel had allowed herself to dream again! Very correctly she mourned Oscar, doing and saying all the right things, and sometimes even shedding a sincere tear when she recalled his 'fantastic generosity' But before the little black suits and dresses gave place to more dashing and colourful attire, she had made her plans. It had certainly been bad luck, after trying so hard, that the fortune which had seemed so certain, had evaded her. But she was young, beautiful, and life was full of thrilling possibilities — more so than ever, now. And, to give them their due, she had to thank the Deans for a sort of charitable modest competence. They had piously explained that their unfortunate Oscar would have wished it. What the Deans did not know, and would not ever know, was that Oscar's widow was in possession of several magnificent horses.

Back with her father, bereft of husband and the social position she had enjoyed, there was plenty of time to think. An old ambition presented itself to her mind, an ambition which gladdened her father's heart. She would start a riding school back home in Rockinish. Meriel was not only an excellent horsewoman, but she now possessed animals some of which might be classed in the highest calibre.

Gladly, at this crisis of her life, did Meriel thank the tenacity of her father's resolve to hold on to Penrose House. The stabling would have to be modernised, but the space, and even the very stone walls, there, were valuable. The town was perfectly suited to her scheme. A riding school was badly needed there. There were no proper riding facilities nearer than Galway, some miles away, and the two hotels and boarding school for boys, besides the convent for girls had to borrow mounts wherever they could find them.

'We couldn't find a more likely

place!' she exclaimed one evening as her father and she sat together after dinner in the flat.

'Jolly lucky you insisted on a five years' lease, Dad! The house should be free in a couple of months' time.'

'Sooner, I hope,' he smiled. 'But I didn't want to tell you this in case of disappointment. I contacted our solicitors at Rockinish some time ago — indeed, to be candid, as soon as was possible after poor Oscar's death. I am told that our tenants can make it possible — for a consideration — to vacate our house, almost immediately.'

'Oh, you blessed angel! This calls for a little celebration!' Meriel threw her arms round her father's neck and flew to the cocktail cabinet. She was feeling more happy than she had been for years, so much so, indeed, that she suddenly pulled up, resuming the demurely pensive pose she considered still suitable, even in her father's presence, and by so doing, unconsciously contributing to his secret amusement. He had no illusions about his daughter. But, for him, her faults could be endearing.

'I must admit you purr very nicely when you're pleased, Meriel! And a *small* brandy for me — must be a bit careful at my time of life!'

'Your time of life! What rot! A bare sixty — and you don't look a day over forty!'

'Here's to dear old Rockinish, then! Let's hope our house will be vacant in a couple of weeks' time! But if not — it won't be long, anyhow!' Colonel Penrose thoughtfully sampled his brandy. 'One thing I want to be *quite* certain about, my dear. You are *quite* sure that you want to return home to Penrose House — well — let's say to Rockinish? I mean — well, *I* couldn't settle anywhere else, but *you* have lots of choice?'

'Of course, I want to live in Penrose House, with you, Dad,' she exclaimed with unusual vehemence. 'Haven't we just been saying how extremely suitable — '

'Yes, yes,' he interrupted. 'And

rightly. No place on earth more suitable for your plans. I only wanted to be quite sure. You are all I have in the world, Meriel — you know that. But I'd hate to think you were coming back home just to please me!'

'What absolute nonsense! Even to please you, Dad, I wouldn't live anywhere I didn't like!'

He smiled to himself, admitting the truth of this.

She leaned back in her chair, thinking of the Old Abbey Farm in this early April weather — everything getting busy there. She never now alluded to the news, conveyed in her father's letters from home of the tragic happenings in the Gregory family — the death of Ann, and Tom Gregory's fatal car accident. There was nothing she could hope to do about it when she first was made aware of this news. But now, things were different. She had managed to keep herself pretty well informed about the Gregorys, and she knew that Dermot was, like herself, free, to marry again. This knowledge was closely bound up with all her plans. She had sampled enough of luxury, and much of what money could buy. But she had slowly learned there was so much money couldn't buy! To her own astonishment, she was realising that for a long time she had been a stranger to happiness.

Now she was resolved to try something different. She thought she could still be in love with the young farmer at home, depite his poverty. She had discovered, too, that there was no actual poverty at the Abbey Farm, these times — that, in fact, Dermot was beginning to make a success of things, that he was greatly admired for sheer hard work, and courage by his neighbours. She decided that she was going to marry him. She had complete confidence in her ability to make a big success not only of the riding school, but, later on, of the Old Abbey Farm! With her as his wife, Dermot Gregory would not long remain overlooked by the important people of the neighbourhood. The future seemed so filled with possibilities, so desirable, that its very contemplation drew forth a little sigh of sheer satisfaction. 'No, Dad, I have not the smallest wish to stay in England! The Deans don't want me — I'm only an embarrassment to them! But, apart from that, I dislike them, and wouldn't live near them for a fortune!' She laughed. 'Literally, for a fortune! No — I'm counting the days until we get back home!'

'Fine! Fine!' Her father stretched and closed the window. It had started to rain. He switched on the light and picked up a sporting journal. 'Er — I've just remembered — they used to keep a couple of hacks at the Abbey Farm, in times past, didn't they? Used to hire them out occasionally?'

'That's right.' She found the coffee cups, and percolator. After a few minutes, she remarked with seeming casualness — ' I hear things are looking up, at the Abbey Farm! My friend, Mrs. Frazer, tells me — in that letter I had the other day — that Dermot Gregory has shown no sign of wanting to marry again. Of course, there's just no one suitable round there! That family used to be of considerable consequence — ?' She looked round at her father moving their chairs to face an electric fire.

'Of the very first consequence, my dear Meriel! Quite as good blood as our own — maybe better!' he laughed. 'Much longer in that part of the country, anyway.'

'Very sad for him, really!'

Her father deemed it wiser to appear not to have noticed any significance in their remarks, and amended, settling himself into his chair and appearing already absorbed in his journal. 'Fine type of chap — very good farmer, given a chance. Got breeding.'

The good news arrived in a few days that the house was free. It took only a week or two to get their plans under way. Cases were packed, the horses duly conveyed to the airport, an route for the West of Ireland, tickets, reservations, and a score of last-minute minutia seen to, by the methodical colonel. Then, with due acknowledgement of the Dean family's courtesy, a correct and even praiseworthy show of politeness and gratitude for the flat, it was handed back to them by Meriel. 'Goodbyes' were said to their indifferent, brief relations by marriage, and the dust of London shaken off their feet.

Back in the big house in the High Street of Rockinish, there was no lack of warm heart and old friends to welcome them. Almost literally, the colonel and his pathetically youthful widowed daughter were greeted with open arms.

A bare fortnight after their renewed occupation of Penrose House, Meriel's father had blissfully re-established himself back among his sporting friends and farming neighbours. Meriel was busy making calls, consulting builders about the stabling, and finding temporary accommodation for her valued horses and ponies. The presence of so many animals called forth the astonished admiration of her friends, the almost awe of her neighbours, for every man, woman, and child in the district managed to get a glimpse of them. This pleased Meriel so much that for the first time, she really felt a pang of loving regret for the departed Oscar Dean.

One morning, Meriel's father knocked on her bedroom door with a cup of tea and the previous day's *Times*. 'Thought you might like to see this!' He indicated a certain page with a smile, and seeing that Meriel was but half awake, he quietly left the room.

The tea was good, and soon had young Mrs. Dean wide awake enough to glance at the papers. She had intended calling on the Gregorys. But instead, on an impulse, she lifted the receiver of the white telephone beside her bed. In itself, the article had little meaning for her. But it triggered off her plan to get in touch with Dermot even sooner than hoped for. In a few moments, her heart beating ridiculously quickly, she was hearing that remembered voice.

'Dermot Gregory here.' The voice, after an initial exclamation of surprise, was cool, polite, but decidedly detached. She allowed for this, however. She had been prepared for worse, maybe a direct snub, or even to have been cut off. She knew Dermot! He used no half measures. For him, it was always a case of 'all or nothing' in personal relationships. He could never dissemble or pretend. And for these very qualities, although she thought them uncivilised, even barbarous, she adored him all the more. Yes — she told herself that morning, I am still in love with him! When has a man's very voice caused so much pleasurable excitement!

She had hated the girl he married, and almost hated him, before she left for London. Now everything was set fair. She would marry him, yet — to please her heart, rather than her head! This, she decided, would be life's best luxury! Whatever the cost, she meant to have Dermot Gregory.

A few days after the phone call, therefore, Meriel rode over to the Abbey Farm with the intention of showing off her best horse, 'Noble'. Aware of Dermot's knowledge, she knew he would appreciate her treasure. It would be a good enough excuse for a friendly opening, the showing off of a splendid three-year-old, destined for future racing. At the hall door steps, she dismounted, very sure of herself, in her perfectly tailored, but not too new riding habit, and looking her best, as she always did in such an outfit. She intended to impress not only Dermot, but his mother, and quite definitely succeeded in the latter case.

Mrs. Gregory was at home, relaxing in a deckchair in the sunshine of that lovely spring day. She was wearing a comfortable old tweed skirt, neverthe-less, and an ancient polo-necked knitted jumper, for despite the sun-shine, there was a 'nip' in the breeze, out of sheltered places.

Mrs. Ramsay had opened the door to Meriel, and rendered silent by admiration, had invited Mrs. Dean into the drawing room, murmuring something about her mistress being in the garden, and that Mike, the cow-man would see to the horse.

Meriel remembered the low-ceilinged, chintzy room. It was more faded and shabby than when she had last seen it, the carpet quiet threadbare. But the room had an indefinably welcoming aspect. Some narcissi, in a Waterford glass vase, breathed a fragrance most lovely and refreshing, and the famous 'Lady On Horseback' hung above the fireplace, a little more smoke-grimed and dim but still striking and beautiful, especially to the unaccustomed eye. Meriel went to stand by the diamond-paned window, admiring the bright flowers in an untidy front garden, and turned as her surprised hostess entered the room, with her most charming smile. She was welcomed very much as she had been used to, in the old days, for it was not in the older woman's nature to nurse a grievance or to rebuff what appeared to be a friendly overture. Meriel's appearance was most impressive. She seemed more beautiful, more blooming, and so much more 'outgoing' than formerly.

A brief few words of mutual condolence passed between them, during which young Mrs. Dean's lovely blue eyes filled with tears. 'Ah, yes, so much water has passed beneath our bridges, Mrs. Gregory, since we last met. My darling Oscar — and your poor Ann! What changes in a few years.'

The fire had not been lighted, but very soon Mrs. Gregory had the kindling wood blazing, as she indicated a chair, and then went to order tea. The two sat down to a most agreeable chat. Meriel was exerting her very considerable charm, making kind enquiries about the farm, and congratulating the other woman on her obvious return to health.

'Really, Mrs. Gregory, you look heaps better — and, if I may say so — years younger than when I saw you last!'

'Thank you, dear.' Mrs. Gregory glanced down ruefully at her old tweed skirt, but she smiled, pleased. 'If such be the case, it is all Debbie's work! It was she prescribed this new hair-do, and the tint — oh, all sorts of things. Although I did it to please her, at first, I do think it helped!'

'Of course, it helps! But, 'Debbie' — who is Debbie?'

'Oh — I had forgotten you never met her. Nurse Holden. She came here at Dermot's request years ago to nurse little Mark, and afterwards to look after me, when I was so very ill. She stayed on with us after my husband's accident, and poor Ann — ' Mrs. Gregory's voice faltered. 'The child was born when the accident happened to Ann. There wasn't even time for a doctor. It was Nurse Holden saved the child's life. So you will understand we look on her as a most valued addition to our family — a very dear friend.'

'How extraordinary! I believe now I

did hear something, years ago — but I thought it was a still-born child — at least my father thought so from some letter he had at the time.' Not sure how to take the news, Meriel floundered. Would this unforeseen fact help or hinder her plans?

'A man is never so good at telling one real news!' Mrs. Gregory smiled. 'Women are so much better in matters of this sort. Mark is a darling child, and so like his father,' she ran on, launched on her favourite subject.

'He must be — er — handsome — I mean — if he is like his father!' Meriel paused, contemplating the toe of her well polished riding boot. 'Nurse Holden — would she be one of the Holdens who used to live in those old cottages at the foot of Knockadee, down beyond the larch woods? Very poverty stricken people, I seem to remember. Dad would know?'

'That's right, Mrs. Dean. That would be the family. The parents are dead, and the cottage demolished. Debbie's one older sister is married to a local young man — living in a bungalow near the town.'

'Ah! I see! Well — this nurse must be quite a treasure!'

Mrs. Ramsay, having donned a pretty apron as a mark of respect to the unusually glamorous caller, brought in tea, complete with the best china and new-baked cakes.

'How delicious!' Meriel sampled one of the cakes. 'Home-made?'

'Yes, indeed. Mrs. Ramsay has us all completely spoilt by her home cooking,' boasted her hostess, laughing pleasantly at the success of this first call.

'They're delicious — and I simply must have another, Mrs. Ramsay!'

'Oh — thank you, Madam! I'm glad you like them.' The housekeeper left in a haze of satisfaction.

'But, where are they? I mean, little Mark? And this nurse? I have a perfect 'thing' about children!' Meriel remarked, her lovely face glowing, and quite unaware that she was lying. 'That was another disappointment — ' Her lip trembled. 'But we won't speak of sad things.'

'They ought to be here any moment. I suppose the fine day, after all the cold weather, tempted them to go further — Why — here they are!'

Two figures passed by the window, the little boy running on in front, and in a few moments, Debbie and her charge were in the room, Mark rushing cold-cheeked into Mrs. Gregory's open arms.

'Nana — we found a daff — a daff — '

'A daffodil! Lots coming out in the far spinney above the Long Acre fields,' Debbie explained, aware of the girl in smart riding attire, although she had not as yet, looked at her directly.

'What a dear little boy — really remarkably pretty!' Meriel extended an inviting hand to the child, 'Oh, and this is Nurse Holden! I've been hearing about you.' The blue eyes rested for a speculative moment on Debbie, and quickly, icily, turned away. There was certainly nothing to fear here — yet Mrs. Dean instantly disliked Debbie. 'I believe my father, Colonel Penrose, knew your people long ago?'

'Yes.' Debbie was removing Mark's outdoor things, catching him back when he wriggled away from her, with practised hands. 'My father worked for Colonel Penrose at one time, when we were small children. Your father used to give us peaches from the hot-house! We've never forgotten them! Everyone is glad he — both of you — are back in Rockinish, Mrs. Dean.'

'Thank you. I thought it must be the same Holdens.' Meriel turned away, dismissing the other girl with the subject. Then she tried to coax Mark to come to her. But he held back. 'Will you not give me that pretty flower then, Mark?'

Mark clutched the flower more firmly. 'No — 'cause it's for daddy.'

They all laughed, Meriel a trifle awkwardly, for the child had evaded all her advances. She had never been successful with children, nor did she like them, despite her assertions a few minutes earlier.

'Well, let's go and have tea by the Aga, shall we? And you can put the daffodil in a vase for daddy.'

The boy's hand slipped confidingly into Debbie's as she led him out of the room. So this was the beautiful widow, Mrs. Dean, this exquisite, well-bred, pink-complexioned, golden-haired creature, so much more beautiful than even Debbie had imagined, a suave, sporting, socially 'top-drawer' girl with purpose in every line of her body, and contempt in her glance! This was it! This must be, for Debbie Holden, the beginning of the end. What chance had a plain 'nobody', like herself, against young Mrs. Dean of Penrose House?

She filled milk into a mug for Mark, answered his chatter, left a note on the fridge for Mrs. Ramsay, who had just gone over to her neighbours' for the evening. She heard Dermot come in along the back hall, and then the bath-water running. After a short while she heard him come down the stairs and, ashamed but unable to stop herself, she lingered at the open kitchen door, listening to the voices issuing from the opened drawing room door.

'Hal-lo, Dermot! There you are, then 'How absolutely lovely to meet again!'

This much came clearly, in Meriel's delighted tones, but the listener could not hear Dermot's reply. Disgusted with herself, miserable, as she had never been in her life, Debbie urged Mark to finish his supper, and then took him quickly up to the bathroom, finding his toy duck and his coloured balls, playing the expected familiar games, struggling with the tears she despised, and not being quite able to prevent them. Goodbye, lovely, impossible, secret hope! Goodbye, foolish, mad dream!

'Have you got soap in your eye, Debbie?' The child, concerned, wanted to sponge away the hurt, and she clasped his little naked wet body closely to her heart. Soon — she must be leaving him. But then, soon, he would no longer need her, like this. Soon — she would be only a memory here at the Old Abbey Farm — how could it be otherwise. Once, Dermot had said she was like 'Pippa Passing!' That was in fun. Now it must surely come true, and the time would come when he would thus remember her — just a 'Pippa Passing' when he had been in trouble — no more, no less.

4

On the evening of Meriel's first visit to the farm, Debbie contrived to evade supper with the family, so that her deplorable want of spirits might not be perceived. Truthfully pleading a headache, she escaped to her room, not so much to bed and sleep, as to face up to an entirely new situation, and to call upon her common sense and courage. These qualities she had in plenty, but now she had to dig very deep for them. Nevertheless, a certain inherent fortitude armed her in advance for whatever the future might bring.

Therefore there was nothing about Debbie on the following day to cause comment. She looked and behaved exactly as she always did. And, as the hours passed, she was surprised to find that his first renewed encounter with the glamorous Meriel left no perceptible mark on Dermot, who went about his farm business and sat down to the family meals in the same rather abstracted, occasionally gloomy, but essentially good-humoured manner as ever.

Apart from Mrs. Ramsay's enthusiastic praise of their unexpected caller, it was only Mrs. Gregory who showed signs of being impressed. The possibility of a new social horizon had been opened up for her, and 'young Mrs. Dean's' elegance, her charm, and her plans for the riding school were subjects on which Dermot's mother liked to dwell during the next few days.

No news regarding a valuer to examine the painting had yet arrived. But, each morning, Mrs. Gregory came downstairs in her dressing-gown to glance through the letters on the hall table, before anyone else, looking for Solicitor O'Connor's familiar handwriting. Even his typed envelopes, she declared, could be distinguished from everyone else's!

'You'll find O'Connor is working on the job, mother dear, and whatever he has to tell us must wait a correctly decent interval in the requirements of the law, before he writes to us! I suppose he thinks we're crazy — as we probably are!'

'Really, Dermot, you are a depressing old wet blanket!' his mother snapped at him, so much like her old lively self, before her illness, that Dermot broadly grinned and hugged her warmly.

The subject of the picture, however, was completely forgotten on a certain rainy day which was to prove one of setbacks and worry out-of-doors, and excitement within. The cow-man did not arrive that morning, being laid up with flu, which meant that his son, Johnnie, the very useful yard lad, did not appear either, as Johnnie's mode of locomotion was on the back of his father's motor bike. There were unexpected callers, on farm business, the man to mend a tractor, and the man to repair the roof of the cow-byre, arrived at the back door, together, just as Mrs. Ramsay had started on a periodic clearing out of food cupboards. Everything seemed to happen at once, so that Debbie, having handed over Mark to his 'Nana', Mrs. Gregory, found herself, in old jeans and pullover, mucking about, helping Dermot in the yards, as, indeed, she had, on a few emergency occasions, been called upon to do, before. But this was no penance, for, as Mrs. Ramsay said, 'the girl took to farm life as a 'duck to water'.' In truth, Debbie enjoyed the work which called upon her to cope with anything out-of-doors. It was during such periods of working together that she and Dermot came closer in companionable, lively badinage, or in even more companionable silence.

'You'd make a tip-top farmer's wife, Deb!' he had exclaimed, more than once, whistling past her with a playful ruffle of her straight brown hair. On that day, he had encountered her emerging from one of the cattle sheds with a fork-load of manure. Stopping in his stride, he glanced inside to see the dim interior newly cleaned and spread with fresh straw. Gratefully, he put a companionable arm about her. 'Is there *anything* you can't turn your hand to?' he inquired, as she dumped the manure. Then, looking deep into her laughing brown eyes, he amended, more seriously, 'And the more earthy the better!'

'Try me!' she challenged, her face rosy from exertion in the soft, continuous April rain. 'Just try me!'

He stood inside the shed doorway laughing. 'I'll think up something!' Marvelling at her willing spirit, he watched her strong brown arms, sleeves rolled up above the elbow, the way her square, firm hands gripped the heavy fork, her apparent immunity to the strong-smelling manure heap. Something held them both there for a few strange moments, observing each other, not realising that they were so doing. Debbie's loving eyes were full of a strange, quiet content, for, always, in his presence, when real things were being shared, working together, she forgot every doubt, and knew only the deep, primitive delight of human loving.

He did not read the adoration in her glance for what it was, yet he had an intense awareness of pleasure in her company, of the 'rightness' of her being there alongside him. On such occasions he knew a welling up of sheer admiration for her sterling qualities, since the day she came into his house, and an overwhelming sense of gratitude. How many girls, he asked himself, would do what she was so happily doing, in such surroundings, wet through with rain, and laughing at her state!

'Not to worry! I'll have a warm bath and a shower and clean clothes when I go in, and I'll be fine!' She assured him, seeing his concern.

Later, when the relentless rain ceased, Mark was permitted to join them. Important, and full of chatter, in his red wellingtons, he ran about between them, so that the three often laughed, and Debbie, noted the sad grey eyes of the child's father, as they lit up with laugher, and she asked no more of life at that moment.

In such ways and by such guileless means had the girl grown into the family, identifying herself with their interests, sympathising in their troubles, sharing in their slowly growing prosperity — and now in the anticipation of a possible visitation of smiling fortune. Whenever she remembered Meriel Dean, during those rainy spring days, Debbie was resolved that never again, would she fall victim to the tearing regrets and despair of the night after Meriel's first visit to the house. She could not deny the immutable fact of her love for Dermot. That could not be changed. She knew herself to be a 'one-man' girl, and as long as she breathed, she must love him. This was her destiny, whatever happened. She must learn to live with it.

Coming indoors for lunch, one day, when rainbows and sunshine lit the mountains round Knockadee with magical lights, and the first cuckoo call came like an enchantment from the wych-elm trees behind the old house, Debbie paused to answer the telephone in the hall. It started ringing as she changed her boots at the back door.

The voice at the other end informed her that he had arrived at Rockinish railway station, where he had just been met by Mr. O'Connor, solicitor, and that they hoped to be at the Abbey Farm in half an hour's time, to view the reputed Wootton canvas, if Mr. Gregory was available.

She could only inform the voice that Mr. Dermot Gregory was at home somewhere about the farm, and that Mrs. Gregory, his mother, was in the house. Then, dancing her way down the hall (for it had always been a natural impulse, on Debbie's part, to dance when moved by feelings, or by emotion) into the kitchen, she pulled the strings of Mrs. Ramsay's apron, so that it fell off at the irate woman's feet.

'There now — just like Mark! And teachin' him a bad habit, too! How often have I told you not to do it!'

The little golden-haired boy sitting at a Formica-topped table eating his dinner, fell into a paroxysm of laughter, as he invariably did, when Mrs. Ramsay's apron fell off. 'She's naughty! Debbie's naughty!'

'You've said it!' Mrs. Ramsay muttered darkly into the sink.

'Ah, but wait till you hear!' Debbie settled the wriggling Mark back in his chair, refilled his mug with milk, and announced her bit of news, triumphantly.

'It *would* happen today, of all days!' The housekeeper stood, appalled, in the middle of her disrupted kitchen, surrounded by stacks of jars and tins, preparing the shelves for Mrs. Gregory's plan of painting them.

At that moment, Mrs. Gregory appeared in a blue overall, with a tin of yellow paint. She had made up her mind the previous day to paint the kitchen shelves, returning energy and health prompting all sorts of unusual activity. When she heard about the telephone call, her face lit with pleasure.

'But — lunch — for the gentlemen?' Mrs. Ramsay's horrified tones had risen to a sort of wail. 'We were to have just coffee and sandwiches, today?'

'Oh, well, there's plenty of home-baked bread and cheese and eggs,' Debbie consoled. 'They won't expect lunch, anyway. It's just business.'

'Don't be ridiculous, girl,' Mrs. Ramsay interrupted. 'We've got to provide something better than that for the gentleman from London! Mr. O'Connor doesn't matter — he's one o' ourselves, so to speak. But the gentleman from London — '

Mrs. Gregory was removing her housecoat. 'Now then, I'm going upstairs to make myself presentable, Mrs. Ramsay. And, my dear, haven't we got lots of tins — red salmon, and ham, and the greater part of that apple pie, left over from last night — and heaps of cream! Besides, there's always a glass or two of wine! So what are we worrying about!'

Half an hour later, no one looking at that pleasant luncheon table in the low, beamed dining room, with spring sunshine glinting on cut glass and old silver, would have guessed how hurriedly it had been prepared.

Mr. O'Connor, a short, stout man, with black hair, introduced Mr. Inglis, a pleasant enough, youngish man, surprised at being so hospitably received. Dermot came on the scene just in time to attend to the drinks, having quickchanged in the bathroom. His manner was as unchanged and leisurely as though he had not been coping with at least two men's work, all morning. The expectations of his mother had no place in his mind, inured as he was, to 'the slings and arrows of outrageous fortune'. Yet, if such expectations made for happiness in his home, he was prepared to go to almost any length to promote the mood of optimism.

After lunch, some considerable time was spent by the three men in examination of the canvas. Dermot handed round drinks, inspired, despite himself by conclusions expressed by Mr. Inglis.

'Aren't you taking something, yourself, sir?' the young man inquired.

'Never touch it. Er — medical reasons!' Dermot smiled. 'I know you'll excuse me. I can, however, take it or leave it, and have never been drunk! Must remedy that some day!'

Debbie was still busy coming and going between the dining room and the kitchen. She had been clearing glasses from the sideboard, and had overheard this good-humoured apology, with admiration. After his father's accident, when she first came to the house, Dermot had explained, 'You see, Nurse Holden, not only my father, but his father before him, were addicts. It's in the family — way back! Two alcoholics in one generation almost finished the Old Abbey Farm. I swear there won't be a third! Not in my time!' She was remembering his words as she moved about the room, too excited by all that had taken place, as yet, to be really happy.

'You'll send for the Canon, o' course?' Mrs. Ramsay had reiterated without ceasing until her mistress smilingly assured her that the Canon would certainly be sent for on such a happy occasion.

At every crisis in the family history, great or small, Canon Nealon was sent for — summoned for his great kindness and wisdom by Gregorys, past and present. A very old, silver-haired gentleman, he had sadly seen the family deteriorate, blighted by the drinking habits and the gambling of the late Tom and his father before him. Nowadays, retired to everything except his prayers, the old man's hopes were fixed on Dermot as dearly as any father's on any son. So it was that in the midst of the afternoon's excitement, Canon Nealon arrived, to be warmly welcomed by everbody.

'Always knew that painting was valuable,' he proclaimed, lowering his long, thin old body into a chair, thankfully. 'Young lady's resemblance to your poor grandfather quite remarkable, Dermot, my boy, quite remarkable.'

'There now!' Mrs. Gregory proclaimed, triumphantly.

'Yes, but that proves nothing, Canon!' Dermot handed the old man a glass of very good wine.

'Thanks, dear boy, thanks! St. Paul, you know approved of a *little* wine for the sake of one's stomach! Maybe nothing can be proved by the likeness — maybe not — but I've prayed so hard and so long for this family — your ancestors built the parish church — ' the Canon murmured more to himself than to anyone in particular.

Dermot laughed his rare infectious laugh. 'Oh, well, in that case we can expect anything!'

'Strange — even as a schoolboy, I frequently observed, Dermot, that you were inclined to accept fortune or misfortune with equal detachment.'

'Birchings and thousands of lines — with an occasional nod of reluctant approval!'

'Exactly! But it was a good sign, you know, a very good sign.'

Everybody laughed, and John Inglis, in this case, exceptionally pleased to be able to say so, announced, turning to Dermot — 'You can have a very reasonable expectation, sir! Of course, I am not in a position to give you an absolute assurance here and now. But you will be hearing from my firm in a few days. Mr. O'Connor will contact you the moment he is in possession of the good news.'

Mr. O'Connor, genial and talkative, stood beneath the picture. 'Let's drink to her!' He swung round and lifted his glass. 'Yes, Mrs. Gregory — Dermot — little Miss Holden, too, I can say with confidence, that fortune is about to smile on the Abbey Farm! And good luck to the Gregorys!'

There followed a session of very happy conversation in which Debbie joined. During the day she had observed John Inglis glancing often in her direction. Once, under cover of general laughter and chatting, he observed, so that only she could hear — 'I say, it's going to be jolly lonely leaving here this evening! Just a room in the hotel — no fun or company!'

'Oh, you need have no shortage of either,' she replied quickly, turning to speak to O'Connor. She had no wish at all to console Inglis that evening, although she admitted he was nice, and at any other time, she would have been pleased to amuse him, as a stranger in their midst. Rather hurriedly, therefore, she left the room to re-join Mrs. Ramsay in the kitchen and to accompany Mrs. Gregory upstairs where she had to use some persuading to get the excited lady to lie on her bed for an hour or so, to rest, before tea.

'You see, Mrs. Ramsay,' Debbie smiled later, 'how little cause we had to worry over lunch! Everyone enjoyed it! everyone is happy!'

But Mrs. Ramsay, who had been treated to a glass or two of wine 'to celebrate', was no longer worried about anything, and moved about her devastated kitchen in a rosy dream, far above such mundane things as kitchen shelves and yellow paint.

'They'll be well-off! Rich! The creatures! An' tis well they deserve a bit of luck at last. They'll expand the place — there'll be no stoppin' that young man! Aye — he was always good an' kind — even when he had nothin'. Aye — he'll go ahead now!'

Debbie, full of unquenchable hope, gaily agreed, preparing the somewhat obstreperous Mark into his outdoor things, and glad to get away from the house for a while into the calm bird-singing May afternoon. The jagged outline of Knockadee was azure, capped with puff-ball summer clouds, and everywhere the cuckoos echoed from the hills and the glen, and far away back of those magnificent Long Acre fields, which soon might be back in the possession of the Gregorys. It was a happy walk, full of dreams and the fragrance of hawthorn, and Mark's lively chatter.

On their return she was surprised to find Mr. Inglis still in the house. Mr. O'Connor had gone, and Dermot had of necessity, returned to his farm chores. Canon Nealon had removed and packed the picture and the men were chatting very comfortably on matters of art.

John Inglis rose as she came into the room. 'I've been advised to take a walk round the farm, Miss Holden! Mr. Gregory's suggestion, but he seems to have disappeared, and I have no guide! How about it?'

'Of course — that is — ' Debbie hesitated.

'Come and have some tea first,' Mrs.

Gregory said, firmly. 'Then you can take John round the dilapidated stables and cow-byres! He wonders, by-the-way, if you will go dancing for an hour or two, this evening?' She smiled, pleased. 'I think you should. You need a break.'

Debbie sat down and sipped her cup of tea. She was not at all anxious to console the young man's temporary loneliness. Tonight, of all nights, she wanted simply to remain quietly at home with Dermot and his mother.

'Do!' John smiled down at her, passing some sandwiches. 'These are excellent! I don't know what's in them, but I've eaten most of them! Canon Nealon can verify!'

Mrs. Gregory laughed. 'Debbie made them earlier this afternoon — dates and nuts and chopped meat — some recipe of her own! Lucky he left you even two!'

'I'm pleased you liked them.' Debbie paused and then amended — 'But as to dancing tonight — I really — '

'Oh, please — don't refuse!' Inglis interrupted. 'I've so far happily avoided my lonely hotel room! It would be ghastly to have to turn in there, all on my own! Have dinner with me — then dancing for an hour or so?'

Dermot drifted into the room on some business with Canon Nealon. He glanced at Debbie. 'She dances far too little, of late.' he remarked. 'And you'll be interested to know she's a damned good dancer, Inglis — the best in the county! She's got cups and medals galore!'

'Don't be daft, Dermot,' Debbie exclaimed, irritably. 'You know that's just for ceili dancing. And there isn't anywhere in the town where we could go dancing tonight — '

'Nonsense,' Mrs. Gregory interposed. 'Off you go and show John round the farm. Then get ready for your little evening out. You so much deserve it, my dear.'

Dermot grinned. 'All work and no play — you know — '

'Makes Jack a dull boy!' the girl countered. 'Why don't *you* come too?'

'I'm no dancer! You know that only too well. Think of your poor little toes, Debbie!'

Canon Nealon laughingly suggested, 'There's always the parish Hall! Ceili there, tonight! My dear Mr. Inglis, you know the old saying — 'in Rome, do as Rome does'. When in Rockinish — go to a ceili, of course!'

The bewildered Londoner smiled politely. 'I've seen Scottish ceili on television, sir. But I — er I've never attempted — But I say, Miss Holden — 'Debbie', if I may?'

'Of course. No one calls me Miss Holden.'

'Well — I can jive — you know, anything like that,' he amended, cheerfully.

'Not to worry! I'll teach you gigs and reels!' she answered cryptically, her heart sore, as she saw Dermot find his pipe and sink into a favourite chair.

There was nothing for it but to

comply with as good a grace as possible. 'Come along, then, John — I'll show you as far as Mike, and he will do the rest! See you later! Mrs. Gregory — Dermot.'

And, later, Dermot heard Debbie's 'Mini' being driven down the avenue. His mother had settled down to study the legal documents left for signing and filling in, her face serene with new happiness. It looked as if things were coming their way, at last!

Incredible! Dermot's pipe went out. Debbie and Inglis — Uneasily, he threw a log on the fire.

'I'll give you these in a moment or two, Dermot — I'm just 'gloating' over them!' his mother laughed.

'Time enough! Er — I don't think Deb was too keen on going dancing, was she?'

'Oh, you know Debbie! Worried about Mrs. Ramsay putting Mark to bed. I promised I'd see to that — and I must go and fix up that young man, in a few moments.'

But when Mrs. Gregory looked up, a little later, she smiled lovingly, and with great compassion on Dermot who had fallen fast asleep, and who looked so thoroughly exhausted. Too exhausted, she thought, even to enjoy the tremendous result of this never-to-be-forgotten day. But, from now on, he would not have to work like this. From now on, he could direct others, as his fathers before him had directed their workers at the Abbey Farm. She smiled a little secret smile as she gently put the papers on a table by his elbow. No — Debbie had *not* wanted to go dancing with Inglis. And Mrs. Gregory's perceiving eyes had noted that even as he had been encouraging the girl to go and enjoy herself, Dermot had *not* really wanted her to go.

5

Urged by his daughter, and because he really had intended doing so, 'sometime', Colonel Penrose called on the Gregorys a month or so after his return to Rockinish — although on that particular morning, nothing was further from his mind.

'Don't put it on the long finger, dad,' Meriel admonished, when the promise of a hot day had lured them both to breakfast on the terrace overlooking a once lovely garden.

'Must do something about it! One should never leave a garden! No one can be trusted!'

'I know, darling, and it's a shame. But I'm not talking about the garden! I'm referring to the Gregorys. I want you to be nice to them!'

'Indeed!' Her father passed his cup for more coffee.

'You can put an awful lot of meaning into one word, dad! But, yes, I'm intending to link my fortunes with Abbey Farm!' She smiled. 'So you've just got to be on terms there.'

'You're very sure of yourself, Meriel, aren't you?'

'And why not? Don't you agree Dermot and I will make a fine couple?'

His daughter did look enchanting just then, her father owned, in some sort of light blue housecoat and her fair hair shining in the morning sunshine.

He sighed. He was rather afraid of this. The house was noisy with two whistling decorators, and out at the back, they could hear a lorry arriving with a load of ready-mix concrete. He had hoped for an hour or so of peace and quiet away from the upheaval inside, and now here was the problem he had dreaded, facing him in a manner not to be evaded.

'As far as appearances go — ideal!' he commented. 'But that's little to go on. Besides, you'll have to work jolly hard for it. It's not going to be easy.'

She sat up, alert. 'Oh? Why?'

'Well — there are rumours around. I'm told he's — er — sort of involved, already.'

'Nonsense! I heard that one, too.' Her hand trembled as she put down her cup. 'Absolute nonsense! Besides, 'involved', if it's so, doesn't mean a thing.'

'For you it only adds zest to the game!'

'This time it's not a game. It's in dead earnest!'

'Not worth the candle — whether a game or a serious venture! This Holden girl seems very well in with both Mrs. Gregory and Dermot. It seems he thinks the earth of her. She's popular hereabouts, of course, so it may possibly be wishful thinking on the part of the locals — sort of Cinderella ending they've concocted. Still — '

'Still, what?' Meriel shot the words like pellets from a shot-gun, her normally beautiful mouth hardened into an ugly line.

'I'm merely trying to warn you, my dear Meriel. I'm sure you'll get what you want — if you really want it hard enough. You nearly always do. But things don't quite work out for you — do they? I mean, the things you've wanted so far have not brought you happiness.' He picked up a morning paper. 'Sorry, dear, if I've spoken out of turn. But I'd hate to see you hurt — again.'

She relented. 'I know you mean well, dad. But we mustn't listen to silly village gossip.'

Her father shrugged, losing himself in his newspaper. He knew the futility of further attempts at caution or persuasion.

Meriel returned to her list, biting the end of a silver pencil, thoughtfully. 'We're going to have a house-warming party, dad, so come out of that newspaper, and give me your attention!'

'A house-warming — ' Dismayed, the colonel slowly lowered his paper. 'Well — I had thought perhaps, later on, one or two nice dinner parties — perhaps in the winter — '

'In the winter! Or next year! Or ten years' time!' Meriel exclaimed, impatiently. 'We're not having a stuffy old dinner. We're going to have a big, bright, breezy, noisy house-warming, with lots of noise and pops!'

'My God!' Her father leaned back in the wicker chair. 'Oh, Meriel — must we?'

'Yes, dad. We must. It's necessary. I want to get old Dermot in a gay mood — I want to get him young again — dancing, taking a drink or two, like anybody else — '

'I shouldn't play about with that young man. He's stern stuff!'

'As I have already told you, old stupid. I have no intention of playing about. I mean to marry him!'

'But, why, Meriel — why Dermot Gregory, of all people?'

'Because I happen to be in love with him dad. That's why.'

'You always want what you cannot

get, Meriel! You've been like that since the day you were born! You ought to know yourself by now. I hate to say it — but you are incapable of loving anybody or anything, except perhaps a horse, for any length of time! Own it!'

'Granted! But this time it's different.'

'Anyway, they're jolly decent people,' her father went on, getting up, for once almost angry, and pulling viciously at some weeds on the terrace path as he spoke. 'They've had years of rotten luck! Leave them alone!'

'I mean them no harm — indeed, quite the contrary, dad. You'll see how much in earnest I am — and you know I'm not as bad as you paint me. Heavens — what have I ever done to deserve all this, anyway!'

'Sorry, my love. I do not want to upset you — I would give you the moon if you wanted it.' Contrite, he pitched the weeds away and kissed his daughter's lovely rose and cream face. 'O.K. I'll call over to the farm this afternoon.'

'You're an old pet! And say it's a

personal invitation — to both of them.' She frowned. 'I don't want the Holden nurse — if I can avoid having her around.'

'I hear she goes everywhere with them, on the rare occasions when they do go anywhere.' He shook his head. 'I just can't see you as a working farmer's wife, Meriel!'

'Ah, but things are looking up, there! And I mean the farm — not those rumours about that painting. Wait till I get going on things up there — combined with my riding school!'

That afternoon, the call was duly made, and an hour or so of reminiscing between Mrs. Gregory and the colonel established an atmosphere of genuine friendliness between them. Mutual family history was brought up to date, and, with a sparkle in her still young eyes, his hostess related the exciting news of the famous canvas and all it was going to mean in supplementing Dermot's financial plans.

'What a stroke of luck! I missed it the

moment I came into the room,' the colonel exclaimed. 'It seems to have been there always — even as a lad I can remember it there! Used to admire that horse more than the lady with the feather in her hat!'

Mrs. Gregory laughed. 'You are of the same mind as Dermot! He expressed such an opinion here the other night! It leaves the panel bare, but Dermot refuses to put anything else into the panel until he has acquired something worthy to replace it.'

'With things shaping so well — and indeed, I see the improvements everywhere, even since I was last here — it should not be difficult to find some inspiring original to replace the family heirloom!'

'Oh, well — we shall not be all *that* rich, Colonel Penrose! Our ideas of riches are perhaps relative!' She smiled. 'The farm, anyway, comes first. My son has terrific plans for expansion. He will be sorry to have missed you,' she concluded, regretfully. 'But it's fair day in Galway, and he never misses that.'

'I should have remembered. But we haven't quite got into our stride, yet. And workmen all over the place! I was just thinking what a refreshment it is to come into this peaceful room, Mrs. Gregory.' He leaned back in a chintzy old-fashioned armchair and glanced about the remembered, low-beamed sitting room, with lattice windows open wide, that warm day, on to the garden and the deep, green-timbered lawn. A bowl of roses on a table near by had brought the very breath of summer into the room. 'Ah, yes, nothing like old houses — and old friends! I'm glad to be home again, Mrs. Gregory, very glad.'

There was no doubting the man's sincerity — for, at that moment, he seemed to be talking more to himself than to his hostess.

'And dear Meriel — it was such a pleasant surprise when she called here to the farm the other day. How lovely she looks, despite all she has been through.'

'Yes. Bless her! Which reminds me, I hear Dermot still keeps up his interest in horses. Meriel tells me he has a very promising specimen. Of course, you heard my daughter is starting a riding school?'

'We did, indeed. She told us about it. What a splendid venture, and bound to succeed! Yes, we have a fine hunter, 'Big Boy'. But I'm sorry to say poor Dermot hasn't had either the time or money to get any pleasure out of him so far — '

'But, I presume, things will be different from now on!'

At this point in the conversation, they were interrupted by the quiet entrance of Debbie Holden, laden with parcels from shopping in the town. She had not been aware of a caller. There was no car outside, for the colonel had walked over to the farm, and seeing him, she paused, hesitating in the doorway.

'Come along in, my dear. It's Colonel Penrose. But I think you already know, him, don't you?' Mrs. Gregory called out.

Debbie put down her parcels and shook hands with the tall, genial man she did vaguely remember. 'My dad used to work up at your place,' she smiled, 'oh, ages ago — when we were children!'

'Not such ages!' he laughed. 'You were a school-girl in pigtails and gym-suit when I saw you, not so very many years ago! Before you went to London for your nursing training. Sorry to hear your parents are both gone, my dear — a lot of changes in a comparatively short time.'

'Well — it's nice you are back again, sir. My father loved the glass-houses and gardens at Penrose House!'

'Those days are gone, alas! Nothing much in the glass-houses, now. Neglected while I was away. My own fault, entirely. Ah, yes — your dad was a keen gardener — green fingers, if anyone ever had. Your sister married hereabouts, Mrs. Gregory has just been telling me?'

'Yes, Letty. She's living in the new housing estate. She has two children!'

Debbie turned to pick up the parcels. 'Shall I bring in some tea, Mrs. Gregory?'

'Not for me, at any rate!' Colonel Penrose found his hat. 'Thanks, all the same, but I've enjoyed an excellent sherry. Anything else would be a desecration. I must go. Actually, I — er — I came across to invite you and Dermot to our house-warming party at the end of the month? Meriel wants to be sure of your being free on that date — a Sunday night, she has decided, so that everybody can be free. You accept, of course?'

'How very nice! I'm sure we'd love to come.' Mrs. Gregory hesitated. Her caller, following her eyes, swung round — 'Oh, and Miss Holden, too! We shall have a lot more people of your generation than mine!' he smiled ruefully. 'It's very much my daughter's party! I'd have given a few good dinners! But that's being very 'Square' and old-fashioned, nowadays, I'm told! We are having a band — Meriel says she has booked the best one in the country! Lots of your kind of dancing, too, Miss Holden. So you should enjoy it.'

'This is very kind — ' Debbie held on to her parcels awkwardly. 'But I'm afraid I have to see to Mark — '

'What utter nonsense, Debbie!' The older woman laughed. 'You know perfectly well Mrs. Ramsay will always oblige. She adores baby-sitting when it's Mark! You see, Colonel, I have been ill for so long, people must be forgetting me. But on the rare occasions when I have gone out recently, I have always had to have Debbie! She's so much a part of the family! It would be simply lovely if she can come too.'

'Delighted. That's settled, then. We shall expect the three of you.'

Thus it came about that Debbie found herself in the most unexpected way, invited with the Gregorys, to the house warming party at Penrose House. Thinking about it that afternoon, she tried to adjust herself to the idea. She loved parties as much as any other girl, but the prospect of this one, though exciting, was almost a matter of dread to her. She was quick to observe how pleased Mrs. Gregory was about the invitation, and her heart warmed, as it so often did, to the kindness of her employer, in such matters. After years of invalidism, loneliness, and sadness, the woman was recovering her old zest for life. Clearly, she wanted to be in circulation again, and the prospect of such pleasant social intercourse was acting like a tonic.

Dermot, his mother suspected, might not be so thrilled. He was not essentially socially minded. But on being told about the colonel's visit and the invitation, on that same evening, he agreed, quite good-humouredly, to accompany them, though without any of the enthusiasm of his mother. Debbie could not help herself from closely watching his reactions. She wondered why there seemed to be no unusual excitement or apparent pleasure or interest beyond the most ordinary, in his attitude, when the subject was broached. He was obviously glad to see his mother's cheerful enthusiasm. The prospect of such a party, even a few months ago, would not have met with such response.

'I'm glad you're coming, Deb!' he remarked, after supper. 'You must dig out some glad rags and dance all night with me!' His kind grey eyes twinkled across the room, looking at her, curiously. 'Funny I've never seen you in a dancing rig-out — you know — floating ribbons and flowers and things!'

His mother and Debbie laughed so heartily, he glanced, puzzled, from one to the other. 'God forbid!' Debbie wiped her eyes. She was ridiculously pleased, she told herself, by these little observations. It was nice of him to be interested and ask her for lots of dances. This was something she had not dared to hope for, and her large tell-tale brown eyes glowed. 'O.K. then, Dermot. Let's opt for the first, especially if it's a waltz — and the last, please! In between, you may do as you please! But you are booked for the first and the last.'

'The alpha and the omega!' he grinned. 'Don't you realise everybody regards you as the best dancer in the county! And for once, everybody is right. Was it those ballet lessons when you were a youngster?' He found a pipe and sat down. 'Ma knows I loathe parties, as a rule. But I like to dance — though no good at it. But it saves trying to find something to say — and if I dance I must have a good partner!'

'The best, in fact!' Mrs. Gregory went on, merrily. 'Did you have much ballet dancing, Debbie? You move like as though you had! I've often noticed it.'

'Thanks, darling! I did, as a child! Despite my horrid, square figure — the most unromantic possibly to be had! And — my bit of extra weight!'

Dermot considered her, she thought, amused, in much the same way as he might consider a new horse. 'It's odd, all right,' he conceded. 'The impression is certainly — er — a little — er massive! But once on your toes and dancing you seem to change into another sort of creature altogether! I've noticed it too.'

More laughter followed these candid observations. 'You'll find lots of girls can dance well,' Debbie consoled him. 'So you won't have to make conversation.'

'Meriel, for instance,' his mother went on, blandly, never dreaming of the shadow she was suddenly casting over the sunlit landscape of Debbie's heart at that moment. In her wildest dreams, Mrs. Gregory had never remotely suspected the possibility of the colonel's lovely Meriel being in love with her own hard-working up to now, poverty-stricken son.

'And, what's more,' Debbie plunged on, endeavouring to forget the shadow, 'I haven't a rag to wear, glad, or any other sort, to take me to such a gala party. Nobody dresses for dancing now.

You just go along in any old jeans and have fun.'

'Oh, but this is different, my love,' Mrs. Gregory mildly protested. 'This, you know, is something of an occasion! We shall have to find two smart new dresses, even if we have to go to Dublin or Galway for them.'

Dermot puffed contentedly at his pipe, crossing his long legs. 'I only hope this doesn't mean a sort of warning — that *I've* got to dress up, too! Because, if so — '

His mother interrupted. 'You have a perfectly good dinner jacket upstairs, white shirts and everything — '

'Probably smelling to high heaven of camphor! If not devoured by moths! Damn it all, Ma, I've got out of the way of this sort of thing.'

'Well, you've got to get back into the way of being remotely civilised, Dermot. That's all.'

'If you mean we're going to be rich enough all of a sudden to move in high society, just come down to earth, like a sensible woman! Remember, I haven't yet received one penny of all this anticipated fortune. We're still exactly where we were a few weeks or months ago — except that I got a damned good price for those calves at the fair today.'

'Pessimist!' Debbie taunted, staring down at her rather worn mule, hanging on her toes. She had suddenly become depressed, the thought of Meriel like a cloud over the sun. She found herself saying, rather irritably — 'You do drip pessimism, at times, you know, Dermot!'

'Oh, do I, then?'

'Yes, you do! This is to be your mother's first 'get-well' party! A lovely sort of unexpected party to which she is looking forward to like anything. And there you go and spoil everything for her.'

'Spoil the party! Oh, come off it! I'm delighted to see Ma getting all girlishly excited over it! What's the matter with you both!'

'We know that, Dermot,' his mother

interposed. 'I think Debbie means that we would like you to *show* it when you are pleased, a bit more!'

'Women!' Dermot raised his eyes in mock exasperation. 'What do you want me to do? Get up and wave flags or something, just because the Penroses are throwing a party!'

Debbie laughed again. 'Not quite! And — to show there's no ill-feeling, I'll fish out your suit, tomorrow, and a nice white shirt and have them all in perfect condition, without a hint of camphor, for the great night! There now! You can forget all about the suit until you step into it.'

'Bless you!' Mrs. Gregory sighed. 'What *would* we do without you!'

'We couldn't!' grinned her son, determinedly returning to his account books.

The problem of a new dress was solved unexpectedly for Debbie by her sister. One afternoon, soon after the chat about the party, the younger girl called at the bungalow with Mark, who enjoyed an occasional romp with Debbie's little nieces.

'You can borrow the new one Tom gave me for Christmas,' Letty offered, impulsively.

'Not the real mink-trimmed one!' Debbie exclaimed, as her sister took it from its hanger in the bedroom.

'The very one!' Letty shrugged. 'It's never been worn. And I can assure you probably never will be worn, the way things are, with another addition to the family already expected!' She sighed. 'So — take it, and enjoy yourself in it. Try it on! Some day soon I'm going to stop having babies and get my figure back — for keeps. But by then, this may have gone out of fashion!'

Debbie slipped the dress on, and regarded a new and hitherto unperceived version of herself in the wardrobe mirror. 'Oh, Letty!'

'See what I mean! Just meant for you!'

'It does something for me!'

'Sure it does. That bit of real mink

— well it suits your eyes and colouring. It's a bit formal — but for the sort of thing you tell me about — it should be fine?'

'Perfect! Oh, Letty — '

'No speeches. It's *your* dress. I'm making you a present of it, Deb — many a dress you lent or gave me. You'd give the clothes off your back, if you thought anybody needed them! Come on — let's put it away in its tissue paper, and have tea!'

They went into the sunny kitchen where they busied themselves with the tea things and buttering bread for the children. 'And while we are having our 'cuppa', Deb, dear, you must tell me what's come over you, when you say you might look for a change from the farm. We'll have ours, first in peace! The children are perfectly happy out there, with Mark lording it over my two, as usual.'

'Nothing's 'come over me', Letty. I've just been wondering if it's time for a change, that's all. I've been more than five years — soon six years at the farm.'

'There's more to it than that, I think? You've been wearing a sort of chip on your shoulder, lately, my girl. So, out with it!'

Debbie said nothing. She finished her cup of tea in silence, and poured herself another, a frown between her brows.

'You should realise when you are well off, Deb!' Letty went on. 'Treated in all respects as a daughter of the house, well paid, every comfort, plenty of leisure — time is your own, actually?'

'Granted! Granted! And Mark, too.' The younger girl brushed an obtrusive tear from her eyes and helped herself to a slice of cake.

'And Mark, too — how could you leave that child? He's like your very own!' Letty wanted very much to say more, but refrained. She knew her sister. One could go just so far in probing, and then she'd close up, suddenly, and that would be the end of it. She went on, however — 'And isn't it nice our being so much together — in our own home country, seeing each other like this — among all our old friends?'

'Indeed, I'd miss it — terribly. And I probably won't leave the farm — I may settle down for another six years or more, Letty dear! it's only that — '

'Restless — a bit?'

'Well, maybe! Restless! And the sort I am, Letty — you know how a thing comes into my mind and I do nothing at all about it — for ages. Then one day — maybe — out of the blue, I decide. And then, I have to *act*, straight away, once I've made up my mind. I hate hanging around, but I have to be *sure*.'

'Yes — I understand. You've always been like that. Remember when you couldn't make up your mind as to whether you wanted to be a hospital nurse, or a vet!'

Her sister shrugged ruefully. 'Indeed I do remember — I drove everyone crazy! Still, once at my hospital training, I never looked back. I had no doubts.'

'Tom and I like you around, Debbie. And now I won't say any more about all this, except — just one little thing.' Letty laughed, nervously.

'Yes?'

'Well, it may be worth mentioning, or it may not. But Tom met Dermot Gregory in the town the other day, and they got round to talking about you.'

'Oh? About me?'

'Nothing very special. But Dermot said you were the finest girl he ever knew in his life, and that he couldn't imagine the Abbey Farm without you.'

'That was nice of him. I do work hard! But I love it.'

'Yes, well, Tom got a notion — ' Letty turned to plug in the electric kettle, so as not to look at her sister while she spoke, 'and maybe I've no business saying this at all, but Tom told me he wouldn't be a bit surprised if Dermot Gregory was thinking about you — in a different capacity, I mean — '

'In what capacity?'

'Oh — you *are* a help!' Letty turned

laughing and red-faced. 'Tom says a man wouldn't talk about any girl like that unless he was thinking of asking her to marry him! There — I've said it. Maybe Tom was wrong — maybe it's too good to be true!'

Debbie moved across to the window. 'Here they come, rushing for their tea! We'll forget Tom ever said such a thing.' So deliberately did Debbie change the subject that her sister was, there and then, suddenly and absolutely convinced that Tom was right.

6

On the night of the house-warming party, the Gregorys were given a really outstanding welcome at Penrose House. Despite the presence of several 'top-drawer' and 'county' people (and these distinctions were still in evidence in the old-world environs of Rockinish), Colonel Penrose, and the by now much talked about, 'young Mrs. Dean', not only greeted the Gregorys in a very marked and special way, but remained to chat with them and take them up the room to be introduced to people hitherto outside their social circle.

It was still a sunlit summer evening when the first guests arrived, and some had spilled out into the garden and round to examine the new stabling and the horses. Flowers and food had been elegantly arranged in the high eighteenth-century drawing- and dining rooms, the dividing doors being thrown open, giving a fine vista throughout the rooms themselves, and through the open french window, into the garden. It was a scene to delight, and did delight every fresh arrival. Drinks to suit everybody's taste were being handed round, and a babble of laughter and conversation made anything but happy trivialities impossible and unwanted.

Mrs. Gregory found herself ensconced, very pleasantly, between a comfortable old friend, and a new, agreeably exciting one. She sipped a delicious iced cocktail and waved down the great long room, to where her son, still with Debbie, had retreated for the moment, to a group of young people by the far, open door, and felt that she had never been more delightfully 'in' things, before.

A band on a raised dais, commenced to play soft 'background' dreamy music, more as an enhancement to conversation, than for any other reason.

The floors, however, had been prepared, carpets and rugs lifted, and the boards waxed for dancing. When a waltz tune began to penetrate the cheerful noise, a few older couples, including the colonel with Mrs. Gregory, drifted out on to the floor, taking advantage of space and coolness before the crowd took over.

Meriel was at her best, a perfect hostess, with something pleasing, it seemed, to say to everybody, moving in and out of the rooms and garden, seeming to be everywhere at once. Her dress was cool and chic, very simple, and just right for the occasion. The moment Debbie saw it, she sighed. Her own valued mink-trimmed 'present', which had looked so right and so flattering, now seemed too heavy and far too formal, more suited to the West End of London than a breezy country house party. Meriel came in from the garden with the newly arrived Doctor Kelly. She smiled very happily at Dermot in passing.

'I think she's probably the most beautiful person I've ever seen!' Debbie exclaimed, unable to prevent herself.

'She's certainly something!' Dermot agreed. 'Doctor Kelly seems to think so, too!'

'Yes, doesn't he? We didn't dream of getting anyone so glamorous in poor old Doctor Christy's place. I say, Dermot, she's coming over to you!'

And Meriel did come across, having secured another partner for Doctor Kelly. 'Come along out from behind those flower-pots, Dermot Gregory! You were always apt to escape into palms and aspidistras at parties! You haven't changed an iota!'

He grinned, unperturbed. 'No — I don't change, do I! You'll have to forgive my gauchery, Meriel! Too long away from good society, I suppose!'

'Silly! Don't be more horrid than you can help! I hope you are going to relax now and enjoy the party.' She glanced round. 'What do you think of us?'

'One has to get used to — er — such

splendour! Seriously, everything looks wonderful! A grand party, Meriel.' He could not help admitting in his heart that when Meriel Penrose decided to be charming she certainly succeeded. Her blue eyes shone with a sort of amused friendliness, and her face, dimpled and young, and lovely, was such that no man, not made of stone, could look upon and remain unmoved.

'You've seen nothing yet! You haven't been out to view my new stables? Actually, I'd be glad of your advice on a few points,' she ran on, 'only, not now, of course! Now we must dance and enjoy ourselves! Later?' She chatted to Dermot as though the other girl were not there, and laid a hand on his arm as another waltz began, and people really got into the spirit of dancing, for the floor was, all at once, crowded.

He said, abruptly — 'Yes, dancing seems the only sensible thing to do at the moment, indeed. But I've been promised this first waltz by Debbie, here! Later on, Meriel, perhaps you will save one for me!'

'Oh? I see!' As though she had just perceived her, Meriel raised arched golden eyebrows. 'Nurse Holden, isn't it? Well, Dermot, *noblesse oblige*! I understand! Later, then.' She drifted away to greet some newcomers, as Dermot and Debbie moved on to the floor.

'You should have given her this dance — since she asked you!' Debbie demurred, 'but I'm glad you didn't!'

'Come on, girl — snap out of it! Smile! Why should I relinquish my dance with you! Besides, Doctor Kelly is far more her style. I'd probably walk on her toes!'

'She's furious! I know she is!' Debbie glanced over her shoulder.

'You imagine things, Debbie. Meriel's all right — up to a point! *You're* the only girl in the world with the ability to make me think I can dance! 'Fascination' — our favourite?'

'Yes! Heavenly!' Debbie began to enjoy the music and the dance, deliberately putting Meriel out of her mind. To be thus in Dermot's arms, their steps so well suited that they moved as one, was sheer bliss. It was true, Dermot was no dancer. She had seen him so often with others, awkward and embarrassed, not enjoying the experience, so that more often than not, he simply abandoned the attempt, and spent the evening, bored, among the boys and men. But with her he could, and did achieve a lightness, an ease which undoubtedly was of her own inspiration and making. That much at least, she was sure of. What heaven it was to be so close in his arms. But for how short a time could it last! Oh, while it lasted, let it glide, let it float, let the ecstasy and the magic of dancing with the man she loved lift her out of this world, into nameless enchantment! Did he feel as she did, even for the brief length of the dance? There was nothing to tell her, even though his cheek was sometimes laid against her own. It seemed to her impossible that he could be unaware of the same delight, although, once more, her native common sense assured her that nothing might be further from the truth.

The music stopped, and the end came. The dancers were returning to their places, or out into the balmy coolness of the summer garden.

Meriel suddenly appeared and took Dermot's arm with an easy casual possessiveness. 'Come on, Dermot — I want to show you things before supper. And it's so much nicer out-of-doors. Your mother is having quite a gay time over there, dear soul! I think she's a pet!'

And Debbie saw that Mrs. Gregory was certainly enjoying herself, surrounded by people and being made much of, for Colonel Penrose had taken his place beside her. It was patently clear to the watching girl, that Dermot and his mother were going to be monopolised for the rest of the night, by Meriel's arrangements, and that Meriel was going all out to 'get'

Dermot, even to the extent of expressing raptorial opinions on his mother, for although such opinions could not be heard by the girl at the door, where Dermot had left her, she saw how Meriel was indicating Mrs. Gregory, and she recalled how such observations had been expressed by Meriel, in other circumstances. She saw Meriel and Dermot go, arm in arm, out into the garden and away towards the stables, their heads inclined together in an intimate, confiding sort of way.

Dancing had started again, a very up-to-the-moment number, now that the party was getting into its stride, enticing the teenagers indoors from the lawn and paddocks. Debbie did not realise that she was still standing in the same spot, completely unaware that she, herself, was being closely regarded, where Dermot had left her, nor that the growing agony of her mind was so visible in her countenance. She was approached by a young red-bearded, red-haired man whom she had never seen before. He was slim and lively, certainly not a country man, for he bore the stamp of the city in every aspect.

'You'll forgive me when I confess I've been watching you for some time!' He regarded her very seriously out of the lightest blue eyes she had ever encountered — ice-blue, perhaps, she thought, only they were too warm and friendly to be thus termed. 'You're quite an unusual dancer! Could I have this one?'

'Why not!' Debbie started to swing her shoulders and her arms and her head, for she danced with her whole body, and they joined the crowd, together, plunging into the wildest contortions of that latest dance, and improvising their own version as it progressed.

'You seemed very taken with those two people just gone out through the far door?' queried her exuberant partner, breathlessly loosing her for a moment, and then swinging back to her for answer, his rather *outre* town shoes barely touching the floor. 'A king salmon being hooked, I take it eh?'

'Exactly!' She laughed almost hysterically, for tears were by then welling uncontrollably in her great sad eyes.

'Lots more fish in the sea!' She was flung from him, according to the dictates of the melodramatic, rather atrocious dance, and caught back in one whirl. So might leaves in a typhoon wind whirl and gyrate, madly, so the two passionately danced the overwhelmingly present discontent of their human hearts. 'Great! Come on! Dance! Dance!'

'But only one king — and I fear he can't escape now!' Debbie managed to observe, abandoned to inner misery. For her, this impromptu dance was a dance of despair — the end of hoping — the waking up from an impossible dream. It was an expression of something elemental, and really beyond tears. For her tears had disappeared when it was over, and her eyes were dark and mute and quiet. The two had made capers unrivalled in sheer dexterity. Lots of young people had crowded around them, clapping and stamping and calling for more. The band showed its willingness to oblige, but Debbie had had enough. She was no lover of 'showing off', and when she realised that she and her partner had made themselves conspicuous, she was appalled.

'Enough? Well, let's sit!' The red-haired man indicated a seat for two near the garden door. 'Perspiring? Mine is clean, silk! Never been used!'

'But what about yourself?'

'I've got another. Always carry a spare! You were crying while we were dancing? Queer things, tears? Joy? or the other sort?'

'Oh, I don't know. What does it matter! The other sort, I think.'

'Thought so. Well, everything passes. Think of it that way — every damn thing passes!' They were silent for a few moments, while Debbie dabbed her face with the cool silk handkerchief. 'Thornton's the name, Michael Thornton. Law student — Trinity. Holidaying with your new local Doctor Kelly for a few days. Yours?'

'My name, you mean? Oh, I'm just Debbie Holden, nurse. At present private,' she amended, with some deliberation. 'But soon going back to the hospital in London where I trained.'

'Pity!' He looked thoughtfully across at one of the laden tables where people were enjoying buffet supper, piling plates to please themselves, and carrying away glasses of wine or cups of coffee. 'Stay right here, Debbie. I'll be back in a jiffy. Promise?'

'Oh, sure! Sure!' She smiled wanly. 'It's being a wonderful party!'

He returned in a short while with a supper-tray for two.

'Now then, tuck in!' He put the tray on a window ledge. 'As you say — it's a whale of a party!'

The food and drink were excellent, and Debbie did as her new friend suggested and felt the better for it.

'More dancing, later, eh?'

'Oh, why not! But I hope people won't — '

'Stare? They won't. I'll see to it.'

All the time, she was looking around, watching the doors, but there was no sign of Dermot or Meriel. Colonel Penrose came in from the garden with Mrs. Gregory, both talking animatedly, and going to a set, reserved table at the far end of the great long room. Almost at once they were followed by the new doctor, and, at last, Meriel, her face aglow with smiles, everything about her proclaiming triumphant enjoyment. She was acting hostess in the most charming way, leading Dermot to the supper table.

'Meriel Penrose — Mrs. Dean, I should say — everyone falls for her? She's quite beautiful, isn't she — quite unusually beautiful — and so charming?' Debbie remarked more to herself than her companion, hardly realising that she spoke her thoughts aloud.

'Quite a dish! Your friends are waving to you!' He remarked, then Mrs. Gregory and Colonel Penrose got up from the supper table and came down the room between the lively groups, to chat to Debbie.

'We have been hearing about your marvellous dancing, Deb!' Mrs. Gregory exclaimed, obviously pleased by all she had heard and proud of her young protégé.

'The highlight of the party!' Colonel Penrose smiled, kindly. 'Sorry we missed it. We were all out in the garden. Mrs. Gregory has given me new hopes for my roses. I thought some of them were dead. But she says they'll revive. Have you two young people had supper — '

Debbie indicated the tray. 'We've had a lovely meal. Meriel is calling you — '

Dermot had risen to follow the older people down the room. Meriel laid a hand on his arm as though to detain him by the table, but he continued until he had joined the group by the garden door. 'Glad to hear you are enjoying the party, Debbie! Everyone is singing your praises! We're just going to have supper — Meriel has something up there

126

— special! But you must give me a dance, soon, Deb?'

'The last?' she heard herself saying. She had not expected to dance any more that night with Dermot, and was surprised that he had suggested it, under the circumstances, for it was clear that he was even more involved than she had perceived.

The rest of the evening passed like a dream, sometimes an unhappy nightmarish sort of dream, in which Michael Thornton kept continually re-appearing, 'clowning' to make her laugh, and while not very successful in his efforts, there was comfort in his interest and friendliness. Debbie was too good a dancer to be left sitting out, and she missed none. She had not noticed dusk coming in the crowded rooms, till all the lights went on, even to the trees in the garden where coloured bulbs glowed like strange ethereal flowers against the red-gold blaze of the sun setting.

The party was nearly over. Several cars had vanished, into the lingering midnight twilight, and people were calling out 'goodnights' laughing and bundling into cars and everywhere praising 'the Penroses' for a really delightful house-warming. The band was playing the last waltz, but there was no sign of Dermot. Michael Thornton again appeared, beside Debbie and she exclaimed — 'Let's not dance Let's just go out to the stables and say 'Good-night' to the horses!'

'Fine! I know nothing about them, but I do admit they are lovely to see in action. Ever seen them dance?' He went, good-humouredly, with Debbie across to the new stabling at the back of the house, in the cool twilight. The horses were standing with their velvet noses over half-doors, because of so many visitors, waiting to be petted and taken notice of.

'I have seen them at shows keep time to music — I suppose you'd call it a sort of dancing,' Debbie chatted, stroking an enquiring white-starred nose. 'Come on, Michael — he wants you to notice him too — the beauty!'

They had not heard the quick step on the cobbles behind them until Dermot was standing there beside them.

'Excuse me, Thornton — but Debbie and I have a date — which she seems to have forgotten!' He smiled as the two looked round.

'I hadn't forgotten — but I couldn't see you anywhere — I thought *you* had forgotten — '

He interrupted. 'If we don't hurry, the last waltz will soon be over. I never forget, by-the-way! And I have requested the poor devils in there on the rostrum to keep on for a few minutes longer, just for our waltz!'

Well — he had not forgotten. Debbie ran into the house, hand-in-hand with him, determined to play her part. She was convinced it was the merest sense of duty, on his part, for he had always boasted that he never broke a promise, however trivial. This keeping of his word, even in trifles, seemed to have become a fetish with Dermot. So, as a good-natured brother might do, he took her into his arms, and once more she floated dreamily, with closed eyes, cheek-to-cheek, around the spacious floors of the Penrose rooms, which, by then, were almost completely deserted.

In the hall, Colonel Penrose and Meriel were bidding the last guests 'goodnight'. Mrs. Gregory was waiting in the car, and in a few minutes the Gregorys and Debbie were driving homewards, too.

'It's been — quite — the most — wonderful — party!' Mrs. Gregory was yawning too hugely to finish her observations, vanished immediately to bed and sleep as did Dermot and Debbie.

7

But the first chirpings of birds in the misty dawn of the day after the party were sounding about the old farmhouse before Debbie had gone to sleep, abandoned to the inevitability of things to come, and the probability of the ending of her dearest, most secret dream of happiness.

In a desolate hour before sleep came, she had, in fact, promised herself to call on her sister, in a few days' time, to make plans for departure from the Old Abbey Farm. Escape from an impossible position seemed so necessary that with the intention of leaving the Gregorys, she slept at last, resignation having a sort of numbing effect, akin to despair. She could not remain with the Gregorys to see Dermot and Meriel marry and that such was not only

Meriel's, but Meriel's father's intention, seemed not to admit of any smallest doubt.

Michael Thornton had urged that Debbie find a place in one of the big Dublin hospitals, instead of going back to London — 'Because you and I must get together,' he had smiled, when they were parting, last night. 'Oh, I don't mean I'm falling in love with you, or anything like that!' he had hastened to assure her. 'I'd never bring stars in your eyes, like you were wearing when you came away from dancing with Gregory! But we could be friends? And dancing partners? I've never met a girl to dance like you do! We could go to the best dancing places in town, and maybe have fun at competitions? Nothing like strenuous dancing to ease the heart and keep one out of mischief!'

'Are you in need of 'heart-easing', too?' she had inquired, amused, but very interested.

'It could be!' he admitted with a comical shrug. 'Maybe she wasn't good for me — but with a girl like *you*, a fellow could forget he had such an organ! I mean — he could tell his mother about you, and bring you home to tea!'

Debbie laughed in spite of herself. 'Well, it's a rather back-handed sort of compliment! But I see what you mean. Maybe I *will* consider Dublin, too.'

Thinking over it all, Debbie decided it might be interesting to try a new hospital, and she owned it would be fine to have Michael Thornton for a friend, because Michael was certainly 'nice', and she suspected that even if he were studying law, he must be a professional dancer in his spare time, or intending to become professional. She was aware, from past experience, that life in any city, could be lonely when one had drifted from old moorings. Anyway, Michael *wanted* her to be friends with him, and it was an inexorable law of her nature that she must love, and be loved, she must have friends and be friendly, she must care deeply for people, and be involved. Something akin to these essentials in her own 'make-up' she had perceived to be also in Michael Thornton, the more obvious, perhaps, since he would always hide the fact beneath cap and bells. How different from Dermot — her thoughts ran on — like a rock or a tree or any force of nature — self-contained, serene, aloof, detached, however kind and 'decent' in all his dealings with people. With the death of his young wife, Dermot seemed to have closed a door on his emotions, an iron gate to his heart.

Little Mark's calls from the nursery next door wakened her, astonished and concerned, to find that she had slept on for two hours longer than usual. Quickly grabbing a kimono, she ran, bare-footed, into Mark's room to find him standing on his head on the floor, with papers, scissors, toy boats and trains scattered everywhere around him.

'Oh, my poor Markie! You must be starving!'

He jumped up to hug her. 'No, I'm not a bit hungry now, 'cause Mrs. Ramsay brought me sausages and fried bread an' tea! Oh, Yummy!' He rubbed his little middle in happy reminiscence. 'Far nicer than old cereal!'

'No doubt! Oh, well, now we must get dressed, when I've looked in on Nana for a moment.'

'She's asleep! I saw her asleep — an' I saw you asleep, Debbie! I did, an' you looked so funny! An' Mrs. Ramsay brought you tea, an' you couldn't wake up, 'cause you was dancin' all night, Mrs. Ramsay said, an' — '

Debbie flew along the corridor to Mrs. Gregory's room, just in time to find her friend yawningly stretching for the clock.

'Goodness! It can't be!'

'It is! And I've only waked up, myself! But Mark says Mrs. Ramsay gave him breakfast. It seems she brought me tea, too, bless her, but I couldn't be waked!'

'No wonder!' As the events of the previous night rushed through her mind, Mrs. Gregory sighed a deep sigh of satisfaction. 'The way you danced! And that nice young Mr. Thornton — Doctor Kelly's friend — Oh, Deb — wasn't it a marvellous party!'

'I'm so glad you enjoyed it. You were quite feted! No, don't get up! I know you like to be up and doing, these days, Mrs. Gregory. But this morning's different! I'll bring you a tray. Mark's dressing himself — even his shoe-laces!'

Her Chinese kimono flying behind her, and still in her bare feet, Debbie was soon downstairs in the kitchen answering Mrs. Ramsay's innumerable questions, revealing nothing of the heaviness of her heart, too busy to be aware of it in any very conscious way, indeed throughout that day, filled like so many other days on the farm with demands and tasks, expected and unexpected.

Like a flash, occasionally, it ran through her thoughts — I'm leaving here, soon. Going away from it all. But with routine chores absorbing her, the thought seemed meaningless. Yet it was there. It would have to be faced, but not yet — not that day. The telephone was extra demanding, and it was shopping day at Rockinish. Mrs. Ramsay was making strawberry jam, because there was a sudden glut of strawberries in that part of the countryside, and the kitchen table shone with clean, waiting jars.

Dermot came in, as usual, about eleven, to attend to his letters and have coffee. He looked exactly the same. But, why, in heaven's name, Debbie impatiently and contemptuously demanded of herself, should he look different? People didn't go about wearing their hearts, or their impressions, or thoughts, or what-have-you, on their sleeves, for everyone to read! Besides, he was asking her to phone the insemination people — 'Tell them the beast was noticed this morning,' he called back over his shoulder, going out again. The calls were duly put through, and Mark was taken to shop in

Debbie's Austin. And, as far as life at the Abbey Farm was concerned, there might never have been a party the night before.

At tea, however, Mrs. Gregory was inclined to chat about the new and unexpected attention she had received from Colonel Penrose and Meriel.

'You were singled out for the most flattering notice, Ma! I'll have another cup, if you please — if there's any more left in the pot, Deb?' Dermot, while incapable of admitting it, was pleased for his mother's sake.

'Lots! And your pipe is behind those papers — where you left it!' Debbie told him.

'Thanks! I'd never find it, if you weren't so eagle-eyed!'

'Yes, indeed,' his mother went on, glowing with satisfaction, 'I'm mystified — but grateful! Not only the colonel and Meriel, but *everyone* — people one would not think of being on terms with — '

'We're going up in the world!'

Dermot murmured, laconically.

'But, *Debbie* was the highlight of the evening! Oh, yes, dear — you mustn't deny it! Everyone was talking about your wonderful dancing, and, of course, young Mr. Thornton. You were both quite sensational!'

'Weren't they! What a pity I missed it!' Dermot raised quizzical eyebrows. 'Imagine our Deb being 'sensational'! Incidentally, did you know that red-bearded chap dances on television?'

'No — ' Debbie hesitated. 'But I am not surprised! Although I understand he's studying for the law?'

'Officially, Doctor Kelly tells me, but Thornton is much too keen on a dancing career to bother his head about briefs at present. He's going to be a clever lawyer, some day, Kelly says. Indeed, I understand he's as brilliant, academically, as he is at dancing. Quite a fellow!' Dermot regarded the girl at the tea trolly with rather more than the usual interest.

'He's nice,' she remarked, asbstract-
edly.

'Yes, but where were *you*, for so long,
away with Meriel?' his mother wanted
to know, curious, but still not in sight of
the true state of things about Meriel.

'Mostly round the stables seeing the
new horses! She's on top of the world,
there!' He turned to throw a match into
the fern-filled grate behind him. 'Full of
congratulations on our new 'fortune!' I
was at pains to tell her that the said
'fortune' was still extremely abstract!'

Mrs. Gregory sighed a little impatiently. 'You know very well it's only
waiting for legal papers to be signed.'

'Quite. But the fact remains we are
still, financially, exactly where we were a
few weeks ago, mother dear.'

'But we're all going to Lakeview
Races this year, aren't we?' she asked, a
trifle anxiously. 'I mean, even if you
can't run Big Boy?'

'Oh, I suppose since you and Debbie
are so set on it, we will trundle off to
the old races, in a few weeks' time. But,

damn it all, it's going to be a poor show — not to have my own horse run at Lakeview!'

'Oh, isn't it?' Debbie said, her great brown eyes dark with sympathy. 'I do so agree! Couldn't we just let him run, anyway?' she suggested then.

'That's what Meriel was saying. They want to call for us — and we are all to go together.' Mrs. Gregory interposed, eagerly.

Dermot, not replying to his mother's observation, went on — 'I don't think so, Debbie. It wouldn't be fair to the horse or to us, to have him run now — when we know his potential — given a fair chance.'

'Suppose we set to, even now, every day, regularly, to put him through his paces! He's in magnificent condition.'

'No use. I did think about that, but I just haven't the time. It's out of the question.'

Mrs. Gregory interposed again — 'Could we get someone — '

'I'd thought of that, too,' Dermot

admitted, with an abashed grin, and since we're supposed to be in the money, soon, I considered I could afford it! But who is there, round here, I ask you! And besides, I want to handle Big Boy myself.' He frowned. 'No — best leave it.'

Debbie jumped up to tidy away the tea-cups. 'Next year, Big Boy will bring home the Lakeview cup!' She paused, putting some cake back into a tin. 'I suppose Mrs. Dean will run Noble — maybe, one or two others? I saw Noble last night. He's magnificent.' She concluded on a little unconscious sigh.

'He is.' Dermot agreed. 'He'll win the Lakeview this year, without a doubt. No other horse in that class, hereabouts, except perhaps the Frazers, but I doubt if they have anything like Noble.'

'In my opinion,' Debbie declared, her face rosy with enthusiasm, Big Boy is as good a horse as Noble — if only he had a bit of training, better maybe! And Big Boy likes soft ground — he runs well on it, and one of the stable boys told me last night, that's the only snag about Noble — he's better on a hard track!'

Dermot ruffled her straight hair as he was wont to do when specially pleased, but passed no comment.

His mother began again — 'But what about our going to the races with the colonel and Meriel as they have invited?'

'Why should we go with them? They'll be a crowd, anyway. No, I think we will enjoy things better on our own.' Dermot very deliberately decided.

Debbie felt her face go hot in a surge of unexpected joy. Was it possible that she had been imagining things about Dermot and Meriel after all?

'Perhaps you're right, my dear.' Mrs. Gregory agreed, but with a tinge of regret in her voice.

'Must be off out to have a look at that Friesian — don't like the look of her.' Dermot knocked out his pipe.

'She's due to calve any day, isn't she?' Debbie enquired. 'She looked fine this morning.'

'True. But I didn't think she seemed so fine this afternoon. Wouldn't it be just my luck if anything happened to my prize Friesian!'

'Dermot,' his mother exploded, 'I do think you take a positive pleasure in being a wet blanket!'

'He is never guilty of wearing rose-coloured glasses!' Debbie laughed, wheeling the tea trolly into the hall. She had seen the twinkle in the young man's eyes, confidently belie his words. 'Bad Rice!' she exclaimed, in the hall.

He stopped on his way down the back stairs, to laugh with her. 'True, indeed, Deb! 'Bad Rice', as the Chinese people say, when things seem to be going too well, just in case the gods get jealous.'

It was a familiar joke between them, and on that evening it had the power of sending the girl happily about her work, not permitting her thoughts to wander to the big question at the back of her mind, not permitting any shadow to dim a little oasis of quiet happiness, of however temporary a nature. No decisions need be even faced up to — yet! Not yet! Maybe not ever!

But, next morning after breakfast, Mrs. Gregory again brought up the subject of going with the Penrose party to Lakeview. 'I'll have to phone Meriel, about it,' she confessed, ruefully. 'You see, I sort of promised for Dermot!'

'Oh, but, there's no need to phone, Mrs. Gregory — why, we don't have to think about all that for weeks, yet!' her young friend reminded her, amused.

'Yes, but you see, I don't think Dermot has either accepted or refused a more important suggestion made to him at the party.'

'Oh? What was that?'

'Well — it seems Meriel and her father are on very good terms with Harry Tomlin, the famous trainer. He's coming to spend a week-end with them, and Meriel thought it would be a good opportunity for Dermot to go up there to meet him.'

'Dermot never mentioned it when we

were discussing this, last evening!' A rapier-like thrust of doubt ran through Debbie's heart.

'He must have forgotten — he didn't seem to want to talk about it.'

'Such a meeting should be extremely interesting — of course! Harry Tomlin — why, he's quite famous!'

'So, you see, that's why I had better phone Meriel — I shall say we must leave it entirely to Dermot. That's the list, dear. The few items we couldn't get when you were shopping yesterday. I don't think any of us were properly awake! But it's a lovely day and you might as well be out, as in!'

Debbie had decided to take Mark for a walk, earlier that day than their usual time for his outing. Mrs. Gregory had accepted an invitation from the Frazers to go to tea, there, and to bring Mark to see the new litter of piglets. The Frazers lived in a big old mansion not far away from the Abbey Farm. But, until recently, the relationship between them and the Gregorys had been very slight and formal. Now, however, it would seem that a more intimate friendliness was being offered, which pleased Mrs. Gregory almost as much as her new friendship with 'the Penroses', as she sometimes still called Meriel and her father. 'I wish you were coming, too, dear,' she had smiled, telling Debbie about it. 'But, another time — when I have told them more about you!'

'Indeed,' her young friend laughed, 'it's high time you got about among your neighbours without me! Or, I shall have to retaliate, and take you along with me, on the nights I go to the Youth Club!'

Hence it was that when shopping was finished in the town that morning, Debbie parked her Austin by the side of the road some miles from the new built up area, and went strolling with Mark down a most inviting lane, like a green tunnel on that hot morning, shady with great overhanging trees and thick hedges. They were going in search of the wild strawberries, which always grew in abundance among the mossy leaves in the hedge banks, along that particular winding, world-forgotten roadway, curving among meadows for some miles until it reached the foot of Knockadee mountain, where it began to climb like a ribbon far into the depths of the glens. Wild roses cascaded from the hedges over their heads, and the fragrance of honeysuckle was borne on a warm breeze. Mark trotted happily with his small basket, optimistically stopping every now and then to exclaim at the bright shiny little fruit.

'Yes, darling — I know — and I do agree, they're delicious! But if you keep on eating them as fast as you gather them, you'll have none to put in your basket as you promised, for Nana!'

'But — ' Mark displayed two lustrous fat little strawberries in the palm of his hand — 'these are for you, Debbie! I picked them special — for you!' His great blue eyes looked up at her, full of sheer beguilement, and she bent, suddenly, on her knees, and fondly embraced the child in a passion of tenderness.

'You are my own Markie — aren't you! And you wouldn't want me ever to leave you!'

'Oh, *no*, I wouldn't want you to go away — ever!' He shook his flaxen head, seriously.

'But now we must find lots for poor Nana who can't come to pick them herself, and who is going to take you to have tea with some nice people this afternoon!'

'I — don't — care for nice people — do you, Debbie?' he observed, after some minutes of unusual silence, jumping up and down the green banks.

She laughed, only half listening, for her thoughts were deeply engaged at that moment. Just why had Dermot not mentioned that Meriel Dean had invited him up to Penrose House to meet the famous Harry Tomlin? Was it merely because he had forgotten?

Perhaps, after all, he had not regarded such an invitation with any special interest or significance, since it could hardly be supposed to have much bearing on his own affairs? She was aware of a sense of guilt or meanness in questioning with such resentment a proposition which might be of interest, and maybe of benefit to Dermot — merely because the idea came from Meriel. But so it was, and try as she would, she could not banish the subject from her mind.

The utterly unexpected sound of the clip-clop of horses in the lane behind them, caused both Mark and Debbie to glance round, standing still, enquiringly.

'It's daddy!' Mark shrieked, in a whirl of excitement, 'an' a lady — that lady who came to see Nana! Come on — come on — ' Before Debbie could reach out to stop him, the child was running away from her, back up the lane to meet the riders.

8

It was, indeed, Mark's father and Meriel Dean, both mounted, and looking quite splendid, Debbie thought, her heart racing, and the same sick feeling of despair which she had experienced at the party, returning, like a giant wave, to engulf her. The two were talking, Meriel with great animation and laughter, Dermot quietly responding with that rare smile of his when he was, for the moment, happy. They waved to the girl standing in the lane, and when Mark ran towards them, they halted, and his father lifted the child up in front of him on the horse, to Mark's ecstatic delight.

'Look, Debbie! See where I am!' Mark shouted, given the reins to hold.

'Hello, Deb!' Dermot called out. 'You must think I am mad! Maybe I am, too!'

Never, since she came to the farm, and more especially at hay-making time, had Debbie known Dermot Gregory to go riding in the middle of the forenoon. Until a day or so before, he had two hired men in the fields working with him, but on that particular day there was no one to help, and the swathes were all lying for cocking, in the fine warm weather. She had, in fact, been secretly hoping to go out, herself, that afternoon, to help gather up the last of the sweet-smelling hay into safety, with Dermot, as she had done last year.

'It *is* a surprise!' she laughed, endeavouring to appear as gay and light-hearted as the two on horseback. 'But — such a pleasant one! At least Markie thinks so!'

'It's a very special occasion, Debbie! And I hope to be back before long. But Mrs. Dean insists that we get going on some training for Big Boy, for the Lakeview Races! She came with some wonderful news just now! Tell you all about it later!' He looked at the beautiful girl beside him with a new look of admiring appreciation. 'Meriel has plans for us!'

'How splendid — but will there be time — only a few weeks — ?'

'Of course, there'll be time, if we start working at once.' Meriel's voice was imperious, for the moment lacking its light-hearted note. She patted the restless Noble on his glorious chestnut neck. 'And no need to be concerned! Miss Holden! My dad is sending over a man to help finish your hay, so that Dermot can come and meet Harry Tomlin. I have arranged it!'

Dermot looked down into the raised brown eyes of the girl, standing, a little bewildered, in the leafy summer lane — those eyes so full of expression, so truthful, that an old saying ran through his mind, as he looked down to meet them, that day, about the eyes being the 'mirror of the soul'. That moment they were full of a mysterious sadness.

'Not to worry, Deb!' he said, gently.

'Everything's under control! And, besides, I know you'll keep an eye on things till I get back — I'm a little concerned about the Friesian.'

'I'll look in on her,' Debbie promised.

'Now then, Mark, my laddie — down you get, and off home. You're in charge of the farm, mind, till I get back!'

'Am I really, daddy — am I really in charge of the farm!' Mark instinctively swelled out his little chest, and stood in the lane with a great air of importance.

'To be sure you are, son!' his father twinkled. 'I must go. See you both later.' He moved forward after Meriel who had gone, impatiently, a little way on before him, under the dappled green and gold of the summer trees.

'Here's your basket, Mark.' Debbie picked up the forgotten article. Excitement had made the little boy incoherent, as he stood watching his father and Meriel disappear round a bend, the two horses breaking easily into a nice canter. Strawberries had lost their appeal. Only farms, and being in charge of his 'daddy's farm', had any meaning.

As he babbled, Debbie picked some little wild fruit and put the berries lying on leaves, her heart feeling as though it must break, for surely, now, her worst fears were being realised. She stood up to listen to the soft 'cooing' of doves in the heavy green of the trees, making a tranquil note in the leaves above her head, and far up in the golden-blue of the sky, larks rose on spirals of joyous singing. 'Beauty, without the beloved, is a sword in the heart'! Where had she come across these words? She could not remember. But they were there, in her mind, rising up from some forgotten depths of truth.

'Come, Markie — into the car! We're dreadfully late. Now here's your basket with some nice strawberries you can give to Nana when we get home. She'll be so pleased.'

Mark nursed the basket, carefully. 'An' I'll make hay — won't I.'

'Well — perhaps.' Debbie laughed. At

the house he stood, troubled, on the steps. Then, looking at the basket, he whispered with a slightly trembling lip — 'Did I pick these?'

'Er — not exactly, my love. But we need not mention who picked them. Just give them to Nana. You *meant* to pick them for her, only you were interrupted?'

'Yes, I *meant* to! Didn't I!' Cheered, the little fellow ran with the basket down the hall, until Mrs. Gregory was discovered coming out of Dermot's office. 'How lovely, Mark! I shall enjoy them with my lunch!'

But when, a little later, she and her companion sat down to their meal, Mrs. Gregory looked abstracted. 'I've just had a call from the colonel. It seems the man he hoped to send can't come. I take it, you met the riders?'

'Yes, in Knockadee Lane, of all places,' Debbie said quickly. 'And we were told some wonderful news!'

'It's almost too good to be true!' Mrs. Gregory exclaimed. 'Imagine the famous Harry Tomlin coming over to this country — and Meriel arranging for Dermot to meet him. The most extraordinary things seem to be happening these days.'

'Great! And he seemed so happy — Dermot, I mean, such a joy to see him really happy!'

'True!' The older woman's face sobered, however, into thoughtfulness. 'But I do wish it had all happened some other time! I'm worried. Mike tells me the Freisian cow is in real trouble. He says we should phone the vet. Dermot told me this morning there was no need for Mr. Clark, and that he'd see to things, himself — you know he studied veterinary surgery for a while — but now — '

'I'll go and have a look at the cow,' Debbie hastily finished her lunch with little knowledge of what she was eating. The day had become excessively warm, and Mrs. Gregory opened all the lattice windows, as wide as they could go, with very little improvement.

In the kitchen, Mrs. Ramsay was in bad humour, complaining that such heat always ' 'played her up', an' it's my belief it's clouding up for a thunderstorm.'

'Oh, I hope not, Mrs. Ramsay — the hay — ' Debbie went to look out of the open kitchen door. Certainly the sky had become overcast since the strawberry gathering in the lane.

Beads of perspiration stood out on Mrs. Ramsay's forehead. 'That young lady'd be advised to keep a bit more distance,' she muttered, darkly.

'Which young lady?' Hurrying into a waterproof overall and wellington boots Debbie was not listening very much, being too concerned by her own thoughts.

'That Mrs. Dean! Over here, enticin' Mr. Dermot away from his work, out on a horse, with her notions an' goin's on — not that it's any business o' mine, to be passin' such remarks, but — '

'Oh?' Debbie smiled, surprised. 'I thought Mrs. Dean was a great favourite of yours!'

'She *was* — when she conducted herself like a lady! But not now! No — she's out for her own schemes, an' the poor mistress up there seems to be as blind as a bat to what's goin' on under her very nose. I may tell you, Miss Debbie — I hinted at such, this mornin' when I saw that one ridin' into the yard, and Mrs. Gregory shut me up — as near offended as I've ever seen her. O' course, I had no right to talk. But I had talked of other things many's the time before, an' never was shut up. I'll keep me mouth shut in future!'

'Oh, Mrs. Ramsay, let's not say anything. This may be the chance of a lifetime for Dermot. He'll be back any minute I'm sure, and then things will be all right.'

'Maybe, a chance for his *horse*. But since when did Mr. Dermot think less of his farm than his horse? She has him bewitched, so she has! There's the big drops — didn't I tell ye' — an' the hay'll be ruined.'

Debbie escaped out of doors. In her secret heart, she was almost shamefully in agreement with the talkative housekeeper, but her own standards of what was proper forbade her to dwell on the subject, with anyone, much less Mrs. Ramsay, before it was mentioned, in such a light by Mrs. Gregory.

She found her way over the burning cobblestones of the yard into the shed where the Friesian was housed for calving. Dermot had left some instruments in a closed box on the window ledge. She soon perceived that the poor beast was in grave trouble. Puzzled, she patted the heavy flank. 'Poor old lady! Never mind! We'll see what we can do to help.'

The animal turned towards her as though understanding and grateful for the human presence and sympathy. There *was* something Debbie thought she could do, to confirm her own suspicions, but she hesitated, reluctant. She had seen a cow calving before, but had never helped in any part of the process, nor did she feel qualified, then, to do so. A shudder from the impotently striving animal galvanised the girl into action. Quickly rolling up her sleeves, she thoroughly washed her hands in disinfectant, and opening Dermot's box, found the instrument she was requiring.

In a very short time she was back in the house, phoning Mr. Clarke, the veterinary surgeon, in Rockinish. 'And you'd better drop everything, and be quick about it! It's twin calves. One is dead — you might be in time to save the other.'

Afterwards, looking back on the events of that evening, Debbie marvelled at what she had been able to do. One went from one emergency situation to another. Work, which normally proceeded without a hitch, was handicapped at every turn. Things went wrong which had never gone wrong before. Some precious containers of milk were destroyed by a 'kicking' cow, usually milked by hand, who refused to give her milk when the electric milker was used. The sky was darkening and the atmosphere so still that every leaf of every tree seemed painted against the copper sky. Trees and barns and outhouses — every material object seemed like objects seen in some tapestry, so still so unreal they seemed, and yet with a sense of waiting.

When the 'Vet' arrived, he went at once to attend the cow. Debbie was requested to stand by, and she was glad to do so, hoping to be of some help, until the second calf was born, but it, too, was dead.

'I should have been sent for, early this morning,' Mr. Clarke observed, testily. He was a clever man and disliked being beaten, even by nature or time. 'We might have saved the two — certainly the second.' He washed at the pump, put his things together, and got into his car. 'Storm coming! Well, thanks for your help, Miss Holden. You're a great girl. You should have been a vet! The cow's all right, anyway.'

Debbie flung off the wet overall. She was perspiring from head to foot, and felt limp and defeated. A quick douche under the pump refreshed her, however, enough to answer Mike, who had been frowningly waiting outside the cowshed door.

'Now what's wrong, Mike?' Her voice was edged with irritability, her temper on edge with depression, fatigue, and the thunderous heat.

'It's the cooler, Miss — the well's contaminated, from the silage, Miss. There must be a leakage. The water's brown and it can't be used for the milk coolers.'

'Good lord!' Debbie sat down on a big stone outside the cowshed. Her cotton 'top' was stuck to her back and she longed to tear it off, to replace with something dry and clean. 'What are we to *do*? Don't just stand there looking at me, Mike, as if I had two heads! What are we to do!'

The old man grinned a reluctant, slow grin, rubbing his stubbly chin, and pulling an old straw hat further down over his small eyes. 'Ye' haven't two heads, thank the lord, Miss, but sure's my name is Mike, ye' have two o' the best an' most willin' hands in the country — that ye' have!'

It was the first time in her sojourn at the farm that old Mike had expressed approval of anything, or anybody, in her hearing. She was amused and flattered. 'Thanks for the compliment, Mike — even if it's a bit exaggerated. But what are we going to do, for heaven's sake?'

'Sure — isn't there the pump?'

'I know — and the pump water is perfect, but don't you realise it's the spring well water we always use for the coolers, and the well also supplies the house! Oh, heavens!' She put her hands up to her hot face.

'I canna' say what we're to do, Miss. Ye' can't do nothin' wi' contaminated water, an' it'll be like that for weeks. Now, Mr. Gregory — he's goin' te get a shock, he is. Disappeared this mornin' wi' that lady — an' the hay waitin' te' be cocked — like a man takin' leave o' his senses, he did. Off to the paddock an' up on that hunter — '

'Look!' Debbie interrupted, springing up, 'We've got to get all those milking cans up here by the pump, when they're full. Get Johnnie to stop whatever he's doing, and help. Then we'll have to find ways and means to stand them in water — come on — let's get going! Never mind the rain — only thunder drops. There's that zinc bath-tub, for one thing. It doesn't leak — ' She darted off in the direction of a shed at the other end of the yard.

But before she could get the door unlocked, Mrs. Gregory appeared, incongruously, in the midst of the yard, stepping her unaccustomed way over the cobbles. 'Debbie, my dear, you simply must come in. Mrs. Ramsay's been telling me what's happened about the water. But, look — there's lightning, again — it's getting dangerous to be out.' A lurid blue flash was, this time, followed by a deafening crash overhead.

Debbie looked at the extraordinary collection around the pump and shrugged. It might serve. Anyway, she could do no more, and Mike, making the sign of the cross, had hurried off to shelter, when more lightning glanced across the yard, and the rain suddenly became torrential. She went quickly indoors with Mrs. Gregory, too exhausted to comment on the state of things.

'Now, then, a hot bath for you, and at once, child!' Mrs. Gregory commanded. She was angry, in a way her young companion had never seen her, before. 'I think it was very wrong of Dermot to go off like that, and no sign of him coming back — '

'It's not his fault, Mrs. Gregory, that everything has gone so wrong — at least — '

'Well, no matter. Go and have a bath and come down to supper. You look all in, and no wonder.'

'I'll do that — but, Mrs. Gregory, we

shall have to be extremely sparing of the water. When the tank's empty, there won't be *any* water, fit to use, except what we carry in in buckets and things from the pump. Silage leakage.'

'I know — I've been hearing it all. What are we to do? Should we contact the plumber at once?'

'No use contacting him, at this stage! I suppose Dermot will have to decide about that? We shall just have to make do, or else have a new water pipe brought to the house from the pump.'

'Yes, but whatever happens afterwards — go and have a full hot bath, now!'

For a long time after the girl had left the room, Mrs. Gregory sat staring before her, unseeingly. She was being more and more convinced that Meriel Dean had more in mind concerning Dermot, than horses or racing. Why had all this not 'penetrated', before now? How could she Dermot's mother, have been so blind and dense and stupid! Lightning flashed almost con-tinuously and the reverberation of thunder round the old house was quite frightening. She rose, mechanically, to close the windows. Rain was lashing the trees and flattening the flowers to the ground. It streamed, sluice-like, down the lattices. Conflict and suspense occupied the woman's mind. She could not ever have possibly imagined such a situation — that Mrs. Dean of Penrose House, should be interested in this serious way, in her son. Hard-working, so far unlucky — mere 'small' farmer up till lately. Added to which, he was a widower with a small child. It just didn't seem possible. And — what was Dermot's reaction? He had never liked Meriel. But was he, at last, beginning to think differently about her? True, he ought to marry, again. It was time for him to break the chains of heart-break over his lost Ann. And to all worldly appearances — what more desirable connection than Meriel Dean and the Penrose family. Meriel was beautiful, smart, popular — interested in most of the things the Gregorys held valuable, and the new intimacy between the two families had been most gratifying.

Yet, now, Mrs. Gregory was bewildered, not to say definitely unhappy about it all. It was one thing to be on familiar social terms with Meriel, but quite another to face the prospect of having her as a daughter-in-law. Mrs. Gregory fiercely decided that she did not *want* Meriel in such a relationship. No — she admitted in her secret heart, and not for the first time, she wanted to keep Debbie in the Old Abbey Farm. She wanted to keep forever, the warm disinterested homely love which Debbie Holden had given her, and which, she, herself, had long ago responded to, by the most sincere affection for this girl who had grown so naturally into their family circle.

For the moment, there was no point in making any reference to it — even in thinking too much about what might, after all, never come to pass.

After her bath and change of clothing, Debbie came downstairs for supper, surprised and concerned that Dermot had still not returned. The two women sat down to the table, long after the usual time, Mrs. Ramsay frowningly reminding them that the meal would be ruined if it waited any longer.

There was little pretence at conversation during the meal. Once or twice Mrs. Gregory glanced across the table at her preoccupied companion. The girl's face was white and drawn with fatigue. A look of strain had banished the familiar sweet expression of serenity. She looked older than her years that evening, and almost plain.

After supper, Mrs. Gregory wandered, uneasily, in search of that sense of peace always to be found by her in her garden, but on that occasion even the garden failed to bring anything but a temporary sense of consolation. The air was cool and fresh, the whole world rain-washed, and although the roses hung heavy, sodden heads, battered by the storm, it was refreshment to walk among them, tidying away scattered petals and tying back broken branches.

Debbie had intended going down to the Youth Club. It was to be a specially interesting night. She had many friends there and quite a lot of interests, but an overwhelming weariness and lack of spirit made her decide against going. Instead, excusing herself, she explained to her friend in the garden that she would have an early night, and this being highly approved of, she went to her room and to bed. Her body cried out for rest and sleep, and her muscles were sore, but her mind was a welter of confusing thoughts. Also, her ears were alert for Dermot's return! Would he *ride* back? What had happened at Penroses'? How had the famous Harry Tomlin reacted to Big Boy? Just how intimate had Meriel and Dermot become, as a result of the day's unusual happenings? When, at last, sleep came, it was uneasy and dream-haunted.

Sometime about dawn she was awakened by stumbling footsteps on the lower stairway. This had once been a familiar sound when she came first to the Abbey Farm, and when Tom Gregory was alive. 'Nurse Holden' had occasionally, risen out of her bed to help the unfortunate man to bed, when no one else in the house was awake, and no one else had ever known about it. Now, out of the mists of sleep the girl sat up quickly, her heart beating quickly with some unknown apprehension. Poor Tom was dead — years dead, and that fumbling sound, so like his father's, must be Dermot — home at last, but too drunk to climb the stairs. Debbie slipped out to sit on the side of her bed. Should she go and help him up the second flight? She had never seen the young master of the Abbey Farm, the worse for drink. There was no knowing how he would react to any offers of help. But a sudden dull thud decided the issue. Whatever the result, she must go and help him to bed. Seizing a dressing-gown, she ran to open her door, listening and tensed, then she crept, silently, out on to the

172

landing, and looking over the banisters, saw there, sure enough, the young man lurching his way slowly up the stairs, clutching the bronze head which must have fallen from its pedestal when he knocked against it — this being the thud which had wakened her. Dermot was swinging from the banisters, cursing under his breath, and the watcher above, somewhat hysterical from the strain and fatigue of the previous day's happenings, broke into a silent fit of uncontrollable laughter, her whole body shaken and her eyes wet with tears.

But, pulling herself together, she glanced across to Mrs. Gregory's door. It was fast shut and no sound came from within. Thank heaven, his mother was asleep. Silently she ran down the stairs where the young man was now sitting on a step, the bronze head laid beside him, and his own bent between his hands.

'Come on — I'll give you a hand.' Debbie took hold of his arm.

He looked up at her darkly angry. 'Go away, Nursie!

'Go away, I tell you — No b — privacy in this house any more! Go away to blazes, an' mind your own business.'

'Do you want your mother to come down and see you like this? Come on! Don't be sillier than you can help!'

'Can't come in at night without some female fussin' an' interferin'.' He was busy removing his shoes, but one refused to slip off, and the other rolled down into the hall.

Debbie took off the other shoe. 'Come on, and shut up! Don't wake your mother. How do you think she'd like to see you like this, you idiot!' She was suddenly unreasonably angry and resentful, but overcame this stupid reaction which she realised was simply an instinctive sense of outrage, because of her very love for the man she was trying to help. Some sense of urgency must have penetrated his fuddled mind, for he obediently gave her his arm and permitted himself to be half dragged, half pushed up the stairs and along to his room, where she pushed him, just as he was, on to his bed.

'I wish to h — Nurse Holden, you'd mind your own business! Who made you my keeper, eh? Like to know who made you my b — keeper!' He tried to rise to pull off his jacket, but fell back again on to the pillow. 'Don't wan' Debbie Holden hangin' round, tying me up in her apron strings! Go off out o' my room to your bed, Nursie!'

It was too much for Debbie. Drunk or sober, he had no right to speak to her like this. Perhaps this was what he really felt — that she was an interfering 'busy-body', trying to 'tie' him to her apron strings! Quite likely all this was at the back of his mind about her? O.K., then — she'd give him no further cause to think she had any such intentions. Back in her bed, lying on her back with her hands behind her head — all inclination for sleep gone, she listened in a sort of dull trance of misery, to the first chirpings of the birds, to reiterated cooing of doves in the great trees around the old house — this old house she had grown to love so much. It was not Dermot's getting drunk she regretted so passionately — that, she felt, was not going to be habitual with him, if even repeated, at all — no — it was his cruel words, and his obvious intimacy with Meriel Dean. The incidents of yesterday, the result of his visit to Penrose House, the very fact that he had broken the vow he took such pride in keeping — to please Meriel — and what other reason could there be for so doing — proved that he was sold to the idea of marrying Meriel Dean. It was the last straw.

Next morning there was no sign of Dermot at breakfast. Mrs. Gregory, completely ignorant of his homecoming condition, concluded that he had slept late, and quite placidly commented that he would probably have a sort of late breakfast or 'brunch' at coffee time, later on.

But at coffee time, he had passed Debbie in the hall as though she were not there, looking through her. When he reached the top of the kitchen stairs, he paused and turned to speak to her, abruptly, coldly — 'Sorry about last night — apologies and all that!' His grey eyes glancing over her, were as remote and cold as stones.

'No need, indeed.' She answered, with a strange numb mildness.

'But if you hadn't come fussing, I'd have managed to get to my room quite all right, without you.'

'Yes — I suppose it was stupid of me,' she answered, swiftly going on her way out to the car. He had not noticed the little suitcase she was carrying, nor the fact that she had placed an envelope on the hall table addressed to his mother.

9

Waking late with a bad head, Dermot Gregory faced the fact that it was the first time in his life he had emulated his late father in the abuse of alcohol. He resolved coldly and firmly that it would be the last. Things had happened last night about which he was sickeningly disgusted. It was not so much the fact of his getting revoltingly drunk. He was no fanatic. That was an incident which, for him, might be dangerous, on account of his family's history. It was not even the fact of his having broken a vow he had imposed upon himself, be that vow wise or foolish — it was humiliating to his pride that he had broken it. What was so horrible even to think of, for Dermot, was the conse-quence of his over-drinking — all that had happened afterwards.

He jumped out of bed as was his

custom, then groaned at the responding jumping pain of his head. But the hangover must be endured. He went along to the bathroom for a cold plunge, only to find the tank full of greeny-brown, evil-smelling water. Silage leakage! Well, so be it! He deserved it! Perhaps, the pump! Too ferociously bad-tempered to see anyone, he proceeded downstairs and out-of-doors, minus any breakfast, to work, briefly and savagely silencing Mike's sly and caustic observations on the two dead calves, the ruined hay, and the water contamination.

''Course, sir, it was Miss Debbie saved the cow — Mr. Clarke said so his self. If she hadn't seen to things in the nick o' time, you'd ha' lost your prize Friesian, as well as the calves.'

Round eleven o'clock, Dermot stalked into the house with coffee in mind, and a need for something to eat. But first he must ring the plumbers to try to per-suade them to come and fix up the water supply with a temporary link-up of some sort from the yard pump. That done, he was on his way down the kitchen stairs, when Debbie passed along the hall. She looked at him as though to speak, but turned away when she saw that he looked 'through' her, as though she were not there, for he was too ashamed to meet her eyes, or to speak to her. Anyone else, he could have casually dealt with, but not Debbie. Half way down the kitchen stairs, however, he stopped and strode quickly up again, just in time to halt the girl on her way out of the hall. He was reconstructing the conversation.

'Sorry about that — last night,' he had said, stiffly, his grey eyes coldly looking above or beyond her. 'Apologies and all that.'

'No need for such,' she had replied, evenly, with no expression in her voice or her face.

'But if you hadn't come fussing like you did, no one, even *you* would have been any the wiser. Stupid thing to make a mountain out of a mole hill!'

'Yes — I suppose it was — just that!'

she had agreed, going on her way, and quietly shutting the hall door behind her. He waited for a moment or two until he heard the Austin being started and going down the drive. He had not noticed the small suit-case in her hand, nor the envelope she had quickly and silently left on the hall table in passing.

Back at work, Dermot had plenty of time for thought, and thinking, on that particular day, was not pleasant. If he could have undone all that happened on the previous day, he would deliberately have done so, with relief. Even the prospects for his horse seemed of small importance that morning, and he regretted that here again, he had betrayed himself, as well as others. He had always meant to handle the training of that horse, himself. He would not have achieved fame, or even perhaps modest success, in a hurry, but one day he would have achieved what he had proudly hoped.

He worked all day with the exaggerated energy of self-contempt and anger.

How could he have been so 'led by the nose'! The sight of the glamorous Mrs. Dean riding her magnificent hunter into his farm yard, yesterday morning had astonished him, and when she jumped down to explain the reason for her coming, he could not but be impressed. She had ridden over to invite him to meet the one man in the world he would most like to meet. It was another surprise to know that the famous Harry Tomlin, the most out-standing and successful horse trainer in the country, was on quite intimate terms with the Penroses.

'Oh, yes, daddy has known him this long time,' Meriel explained. 'He is having dinner with us, tonight, to meet a few of our racing and sporting friends — mostly daddy's affair, but I've been telling Harry Tomlin about your horse — so he wants to see him! *And you*, of course!'

'You can't be really serious — I mean I should be honoured, but Harry Tomlin wanting to see Big Boy — come now — you can't be serious!'

'Never more so! You — and I, believe that horse of yours has got something far above average? Right?'

'Oh, sure! Sure!'

'If we once get Tomlin's interest, you're made!'

To give himself time, Dermot excused himself to wash his hands at the pump. If this were genuine — and surely it must be genuine — could he possibly afford to refuse such an extraordinary opportunity? He'd be mad to refuse it? He dried his hands with some deliberation. He had just been on his way into the shed to see his much prized Friesian, but Meriel's astounding invitation had banished even this important concern out of mind, for the moment. There, Meriel stood astride on the cobbled yard, her blue eyes blazing with excitement and enticement, waiting for his answer.

'Look here — why should you do this for me?' he asked, bluntly. And then, not waiting for what she might say, he went on — 'Do you realise that, supposing such a miracle happened, and suppose Big Boy ran at Lakeview, you will jeopardise your own chances! Because, I'm pretty certain if he really got going, he'd beat even this fine fellow!' He patted the gleaming arch of Meriel's Noble. 'I'll lay odds on it!'

'Doubtless!' she agreed, breezily. 'Although that's debatable! But that's the fun of the whole thing, isn't it? Your horse is a worthy competitor. I know his potential. And except for Frazers' — there isn't an outstanding runner for the Lakeview. There's no sport, unless there's suspense, now, is there?'

'That's true.'

'So what are we waiting for? Come on, and get Big Boy, and we'll ride across and see what happens? We can have a bit of try-out in Knockadee Lane.'

'It's crazy — I've no right to leave just now — '

She interrupted. 'Don't be absurd. You're being offered an opportunity which probably won't come your way again. You should always rise to an opportunity! You slave, Dermot!'

'Maybe — in your opinion. But I don't look on my job here as slavery. I enjoy every damn moment of it, Mrs. Dean.'

'Now I've put my foot in it and said the wrong thing — '

'Not at all!' He grinned, repentant, seeing the real distress in her lovely face. She cared, then — this strange creature really *cared* to see his horse brought forward! 'Let's go! Only, I have a phone call to make. My Friesian's in trouble, calving.'

'O.K. But do hurry, Dermot, because we have so much to do, you know! Oh, and by-the-way, my dad says he will send over a man, Reynolds, to haymake for you.'

'Great!' They went quickly into the house, Dermot to his office where he found the line engaged, and having waited some time he had to leave a message, not too happy in his mind about it.

'Won't be a moment changing,' he said, in the hall. 'Can't go out like this! Wait in here.' He opened the sitting-room door, and vanished upstairs, two or three steps at a time.

Meriel waited, a little impatiently in the familiar sunny room, but she was joined almost immediately by Mrs. Gregory who was as much surprised as Dermot had been, when she heard the reason for such an early call.

More than ever convinced that there was more in all this attention than horses, Dermot's mother marvelled. That this vibrant, glamorous blue-blooded creature standing by the open lattice window, tapping her leather boot with her crop, so almost overpoweringly sure of herself — that this young woman should be interested in Dermot, was almost unbelievable. Could she be really in love with him? Why was it? What was really happening in Meriel's mind?

'You'll have some sherry?' Mrs. Gregory, recollecting herself, offered.

'Thanks. Not now. Another time. We are rather in a hurry. Ah — here he comes!'

They were mounted and gone before Mrs. Gregory had fully realised what was happening. She watched them from the windows ride down the drive, until, before disappearing through the gate, Dermot turned to wave back at her, as also did his companion. What a splendid couple they looked. Why could she not be content to stand by and let destiny take its course? What was the use of interference or wishful thinking, or even the most well-intentioned advice? Everyone must plough his or her own furrow in life. Would it not be the height of folly to try to persuade them otherwise? Especially young people — were they not entitled to decisions of their own making?

Meanwhile, as Debbie began to cope with things at the Abbey Farm that day and despite the thunderstorm, exciting things were taking place in, and around Penrose House. As soon as the storm passed, everybody there seemed glad to wander out of doors again to the interesting business of the party. Harry Tomlin had, earlier, put Dermot's horse through his paces — it being obvious to everyone, and acutely so to Dermot, himself, that Tomlin was doing so merely to please his enchanting hostess. But, later, in the coolness of the rain-washed afternoon, while the other racing men and women strolled out into the paddocks after lunch, to see and some to ride other horses, it became apparent that Harry Tomlin was becoming really interested in Big Boy, and the trainer's lean, brown face became quite serious with a look of intense concentration. He swung himself up, easily and lightly into the saddle. 'Back in half an hour, or so, Meriel!' he called out, trotting the horse down the near paddocks and away out of sight into the far fields.

Colonel Penrose came over to where Dermot was watching the performance from the steps of the house. 'You're in luck, Gregory!' he declared, impressed. 'Once Harry goes off like that, he's sold!' He then turned to introduce Dermot to some people who had just arrived. 'I don't think you have met the Hennessys — do come along in, everybody, and have a drink.'

After a while, it seemed to Dermot that the room was over-crowded with people, some sporting and racing men and women he knew of, or about — some few he was already on friendly terms with. It was all very pleasant — not to say exhilarating — for a while. But being no lover of parties, and having no flair for amusing small talk, he soon began to feel both bored and uncomfortable among all these rather smart people — svelte young women, and dapper young men — all Meriel's friends, and different, not only in appearance, but in manner tone, speech, and outlook. He could easily distinguish the colonel's middle-aged friends, genuine horse-lovers and sportsmen of a more rugged, down-to-earth type, with whom he felt much more 'at home'. Speculating as to *why* — just *why* Meriel was doing all this for him, why she had included him among these people, why she had secured Tomlin's interest in his horse, he stood apart, awkwardly. Was it possible that this extraordinary young woman was really 'in love' or supposing herself to be falling in love with him? Gregory while having a sensible estimation of himself, as a man, had no trace of vanity in his make-up, hence his bewilderment.

A little later, Meriel came into the drawing room, gaily, possessively taking hold of his arm. 'I'm so glad for you, Dermot! Harry has just come back — and I believe all's well for Big Boy! I hoped for this! I knew it must be, in fact!'

'Thanks, Meriel. I find it hard to take all this in — and I cannot imagine why you are doing this for me! But,' he went on quickly, not waiting for an answer, 'if Tomlin does concern himself with my horse, I guess it will mean I'll have to fork up some pretty hefty fees!'

'Not so hefty, I promise! Anyway, you'll get it all back with interest! And, don't forget, you're not a poor man any more,' she concluded, laughing. 'You can afford it!'

'Perhaps!' he smiled. 'But I assure you, Meriel, even if my best expectations are realised — I am not going to be a *rich* man — ever! In your estimation! I have no flair for money-making!'

'That's just why I — er — that's just why I like you so very, very much, Dermot! You're different!'

He turned away from the expression in her bold blue eyes. It was impossible, despite his convictions about her, not to be attracted, and especially by her engaging enthusiasm. Had he, perhaps, been a bit prejudiced and hard on Meriel? Had he misjudged her — holding out on her by a priggish attitude of unforgiving inflexibility? Or — was he being swept off his feet, so to speak, by this whole unexpected whirlwind event?

He saw her being claimed by some other people with a sense of relief. He wanted to think — to be sure that there was no hidden snag in all this. Standing there among all those well-to-do 'horsey' people, not really belonging to her 'set', he asked himself, repeatedly, what sort of a person was Meriel Dean — besides being such a charmer — such an enchantress? Obviously, Tomlin was infatuated by her, and Tomlin was a very rich man. These speculations raced like lightning through his mind as he stood, occasionally talking, if he were approached, but awkwardly, uncomfortably, wishing this damned social cocktail party or whatever it was, were over.

Then, suddenly, he felt Meriel's arm again slipping into his own. She was radiant. 'Listen — great news. Harry is back — ' A maid passed by with a small silver tray, and Meriel, playfully, took it from her, while she, herself, mixed a drink for the trainer, who had just entered the room. She handed Tomlin the drink, and tossed off her own. 'Come on — spare us any more suspense, Harry! What's the verdict?'

Tomlin sampled his drink, his eyes admiringly on the lady's face. But he turned at once to lay a firm hand on Dermot's shoulder. 'A great horse, Gregory. In fact — I make bold to say he will go far — though, as you know, there's no absolute guarantee about such a temperamental animal as a thoroughbred. But I'm prepared — in fact — I would *like* to take him on, if you'd like that? I'd say he will be heard of!'

'Of course, sir, I'm scarcely able to grasp such a wonderful bit of luck!'

'Oh, congratulations, Dermot!' Meriel exclaimed. 'Daddy, did you hear — Harry is going to train Dermot's horse! Big Boy will run at Lakeview, after all, to begin with! Our Noble will have to look to his laurels!'

Everybody seemed to have heard her delighted words. Dermot found himself surrounded by a crowd of wellwishers, sportsmen, jockeys, a certain titled woman from the adjoining county who owned a famous race-horse — people who were individually intensely interesting, but who, en masse, were overwhelming.

'The Gregorys were always a fine old family! Got breeding!' The colonel observed, very pleased at the success of his daughter's plans. 'You must have it in you somewhere, my boy! Bound to come out!'

'Don't confuse my character — a questionable affair — with my horse, sir!' Dermot laughed, cryptically.

'I say — everybody — let's all drink to Big Boy!' Meriel invited, her blue laughing glance including Dermot, as she handed him a brimming glass of champagne. 'Come on, old Frostie! This is a special occasion, for heaven's sake! Harry Tomlin surely deserves a toast, doesn't he?' Meriel's bright eyes as well as her mocking voice, challenged him.

The trainer politely lifted his glass, having no idea of what was involved, but Colonel Penrose hesitated, then tipped his glass against Dermot's. Everybody was congratulatory and everybody was drinking. Then, almost mechanically, not wishing to offend, or to seem priggish, on this, of all, occasions, Dermot lifted his glass and frankly enjoyed the excellent champagne.

Afterwards, he could not quite remember how that afternoon slipped away. There had to be some important business arrangements between Harry Tomlin, and himself, and Meriel. The horse was to be conveyed to Meath that evening, and the horse-box made ready. People came and went in and out of the house, all with something to chat about, and drinks were being served most of the time. Occasionally, Dermot paused to glance at the clock, then at his wristwatch, unbelievingly. He heard himself declaring that he must get back home, but, somehow, he did not go. As in a frustrating dream, something, or someone, always just prevented him from getting free.

But suddenly it was tea time, and people separated, dispersed, and drove away. Only a few ladies remained in a group for tea in the drawing room. Meriel had changed out of her habit and wore a pretty festive dress.

'You and I are going celebrating, Dermot!' She laughed, and then went on, in a coaxing whisper — 'a little place I know out in the country where we can have dinner and dance — very special! Come on! Get in! I'll drive!'

Dermot knew that he had taken too much to drink. He felt dazed and bemused and incapable. He would do as she suggested, he decided, vaguely telling himself that a drive with the car window open would sober him enough to appear at home as usual, even if late. Harry Tomlin seemed to have left, having promised to keep in touch with the Abbey Farm by phone, during the next few weeks. Well — that much had been achieved, and soon, he, Dermot, would get away from this maddeningly attractive, insistent creature beside him. That he found her physically attractive there was no denying, but this ephemeral intoxication could be compared, as far as he was concerned, with that produced by too much to drink. For him, it was of no more importance. Yet it was there, and even in his fuddled state, he wanted to get away from it.

But after dinner, in bemused intimacy, with soft lights and dancing, he found himself unable and even unwilling to leave Meriel. He was almost angrily aware that her attitude towards him had gradually changed. Or was he imagining that she was mocking at — laughing *at* him, rather than *with* him?

They wandered out into the hotel garden. It was dusk — almost dark, and the summer air was fragrant with the perfume of flowers and grasses. It was impossible to resist Meriel's inviting, laughing lips, her provocative nearness, until, in the shade of some dim cypress trees, she raised her beautiful bare arms and twined them about his neck, drawing his face down to hers. Sitting together in the bower of trees, he found himself, at last, wildly refusing to let her go. How long they had been there he did not know, nor to what extent his love-making had caused her laughing escape. Desire and anger had made him almost mad, for the moment, and there was a fierce element of anger in his lovemaking, for he knew himself helpless and trapped, and he knew also that Meriel was laughing at him, because she had got him exactly where she wanted him. Then she escaped, and disappeared like a white shadow, between the trees into the lighted ballroom and the dancing and music.

He remained sitting where he was, searching in vain for cigarettes in his pockets, incapable of coherent thought, except that he knew he was drunk, impossibly drunk, and ferociously angry, and that he had behaved like a cad. Yet, strangely, it was not so much that he had made violent love to a young woman whom he neither respected nor cared for, but that he had sunk to a level beyond even the betrayal of his principles — he had betrayed someone — whom had he betrayed?

He rose to stagger about in the semi-darkness, and turned abruptly when a quick strong hand was placed on his shoulder.

'Black coffee, eh?' It was a grim-visaged Harry Tomlin.

Surprised, Dermot exclaimed, thickly — 'But you went back home to Meath — '

'Your horse did. But I guessed I'd be wanted hereabouts. Have to keep an eye on my property, you know! I've more on hand than horses to train and tame, Gregory! The way I feel right now is that I could bash your face in — only I know how things happen. Come on — this way.' He pushed the younger man in front of him with little attempt at gentleness, into an annex of the hotel kitchen. 'Sit down. Drink that! I'll drive you home.'

Dermot drank the coffee, glaring at Tomlin the while. 'So — you'd bash my face in, would you? Take care, Tomlin — there'd be more than one face in a pretty sorry condition — '

'Finish the coffee. Sorry. I shouldn't have said that — but I'm in a damned hurry. I've to get back to Meath. Important business in a few hours' time — it's nearly three o'clock. Her father has taken Mrs. Dean home, and not before it was time.'

'I see.' Dermot got into the car and was silent until they reached the drive gates of the Abbey Farm. Then he inquired, with grave deliberation — 'Did I dream all that about my horse — about your training my horse?'

'No — *that's* real! He's over in my stables by now — long ago.'

'I see.' The coffee had cleared Dermot's head somewhat, but he had to be helped out of the car.

'Can you make the drive on foot?'

'To be sure I can make the drive, man, what are you talking about! It's fine of you, Mr. Tomlin. It would have been great. But you'd best send him right back here, at once, the horse.'

'Indeed? Why?'

'Because I'd be under a compliment to — to — '

'Mrs. Dean!'

'Aye — '

'Compliment be damned! Don't worry about that lady! Go home to bed.'

Harry turned the car and vanished down the road before Dermot had succeeded in closing the gate. It was a long time before he managed to reach the hall door, and then to find the key, and afterwards to climb the stairs. He hadn't realised he was so near the bronze head, when it fell off its pedestal — and damn — there was Debbie — Debbie — Debbie — Betrayal! *That* was it — He sat on the step of the stairs. He knew he had betrayed *someone* — now he knew — *Debbie*.

10

Her sister would like to have kept Debbie with her for some time, for many reasons, but it was clear that the younger girl was eager to be off next morning, to Dublin, where she had already phoned the matron of one of the largest hospitals, for an interview. Immediately after an early breakfast, therefore, on the morning after leaving the Abbey Farm, she boarded the city-bound train, checked in at a 'Bed and Breakfast' place in the suburbs, dropped into a popular oriental cafe in Grafton Street for a light lunch of coffee and rolls and cheese, and was at the hospital some quarter of an hour or so before the appointed time.

The moment she stepped into the hospital corridors, Debbie assumed another, dormant aspect of her personality, a sort of second skin, which brought a certain sense of security and 'rightness'. This had nothing to do with being happy or sad, or, indeed, with the emotions in any respect. She waited, alert, calm, and resigned in Matron's office, until that busy, bustling woman appeared.

'Sit down, my dear. Nurse Holden, isn't it? I have had a telephone conversation with your matron at the London hospital. By all accounts, you are a first-class nurse!'

Debbie smiled. 'I hope so. I like nursing. And you will have a testimonial from the people where I have been doing private nursing for the past five years, just as soon as they are requested to get in touch with you. And — these, here — ' She withdrew a roll of envelopes from a little bag slung over her shoulder.

'Yes, yes.' Matron glanced through the papers and certificates with cursory interest. She had heard enough, and now, looking at the girl, had already seen enough, to be confident. 'I think it's just a matter of when you can come to us, Nurse Holden? We can do with you!'

Debbie put the papers back into her bag. 'I can come at once, Matron, whenever you wish, in fact.'

'Good! What about straight away? Tomorrow?'

'That will suit me fine.'

'You must see something of our nurses' quarters and the hospital, generally. We rather pride ourselves upon being very up-to-date!' Debbie followed the friendly woman along corridors, into wards, theatre and the Nurses' quarters.

She liked all she saw that day, not excluding matron, and then spent the afternoon in the near-by public library, writing letters to a few of her friends back home to enlighten them about what might seem a very sudden decision on her part. Beyond a brief reference to the happy five years at the farm with the Gregorys, and that she considered it was time for a change, she made no attempt at explanation. What she had done was normal and reasonable, and would cause no particular comment.

After some hesitation, later, in a little tea-shop, she 'phoned a city number, consulting her diary before doing so to find the number, and when a woman's voice answered that this was Mrs. Thornton speaking, Debbie inquired with much more casualness than she felt, if Michael were about.

'This moment come in! Do you want to speak to him? And whom shall I say?'

'Er — Debbie Holden, Rockinish.'

'Hold on, please.'

Debbie held on, and in a few moments the exuberant tones of her dancing friend was greeting her with unfeigned pleasure.

'Talk about 'a tide in the affairs of men' — I can't believe it!' he exclaimed. 'The very girl I was thinking of! That was my parent — my mother — speaking to you just now. She can verify that I had mentioned your name this very morning at breakfast! Fantastic!'

'Just as crazy as ever!' Debbie observed, amused and warmed at heart by such a genuine welcome. 'But what on earth are you talking about?'

'Listen — where are you? Can I get to you? Can you drop everything, for tonight?'

'I'm in a kiosk on O'Connell Street. I'm starting work at St. Mary's Hospital, tomorrow. And, except for my handbag, I've nothing to drop!'

'Great! Great! Listen — can you grab a 120A bus, there opposite you? Get off at Woodbine Avenue, Avonlea? Ours is number seventeen, semi-detached, can't mistake us! Usual grass plot, flower-bed in the middle, green garage, net curtains — the lot! As I say — you can't mistake us! Go across *now* and jump on the bus — you'll be just in time for a nice meal!'

'Thanks — I'll do that, though the queue is about a mile long! But go ahead with your meal, because I've just had tea.'

'Even so! There's a good service. Expect you in about twenty minutes. I've heaps to say to you — and it won't wait!'

Intrigued and decidedly cheered, Debbie emerged from the kiosk, glanced at her wrist-watch, waited in the line for the next surge of pedestrian crossing, and found a place in the queue.

In a little over the suggested 'twenty minutes', she was on the doorstep of number seventeen, Woodbine Avenue, putting a forefinger on a chiming bell. The woman who opened the door was unmistakably the mother of her friend. Her reddish hair was streaked with grey, but, otherwise, the cheery countenance, the blue eyes, the light figure, the engaging manner, marked her as inevitably the sort of woman who must be Michael's mother. She admitted to it, and in the most friendly way, invited the girl inside. As they stood for a moment in the hall, the bathroom door upstairs opened, and Michael, himself dripping wet and partly encased in a bath towel, appeared on the carpeted landing. Bare-footed, he ran down the stairs to implant a cool, wet kiss on Debbie's cheek, and to whirl her into the dining room in a dance of welcome.

'Just having a bath and brush-up. Be down in a moment. Tell you everything then. Give her something good to eat, Angel-mum!'

'Mad! Quite mad!' Mrs. Thornton shrugged. 'But do sit down, Miss Holden, and even if you've had tea — there's a nice mushroom and chicken casserole in the oven. We always have a sort of high tea — it's no good waiting till later for a meal because Michael is never at home then, and he has to eat, you know, sometimes! I have to see to that!'

'Well — ' her caller laughed. 'I must admit my tea was merely a pot of tea and a biscuit — so I can do with a bit of that delicious smelling thing in the oven — if you can spare it.'

'Of course — lots for us all.' Mrs.

Thornton sat down, her chin in her hand, looking thoughtfully at Debbie. 'You see, Miss Holden, his dancing partner, the young lady with whom he always dances on television, has been whipped off to hospital — this morning it happened — to have her appendix removed. Poor girl — but, yes, she's quite 'comfortable', they tell us, and has had her operation. But she will be out of circulation for some time, naturally, and Michael is at his wit's end. He doesn't hit it off with her substitute!'

'Oh — ?'

'Only this morning,' Mrs. Thornton ran on, 'he was saying to me 'if only I could grab that girl over there from the West, quiet sort with brown eyes — wouldn't ever guess to look at her — ' ' She laughed. 'I quote, Miss Holden! Those were his exact words! Wasn't it extraordinary your phoning! But he must have got in touch with you? How else — '

'No, he didn't, Mrs. Thornton. Anyway, I was at my sister's house last night, so he couldn't have!'

'Well, upon my word, I've never believed in 'Fate' or 'Destiny', or that sort of thing, before! But there must be something in it, Miss Holden. There really must!' Mrs. Thornton concluded, awed.

'But, do you mean he is going to ask me to dance on television with him, tonight?' Debbie's dark eyes were enormous with amazement. Her face had paled a little with excitement, and then flushed with sudden nervous reaction. 'He couldn't! He's crazy! Anyway, I wouldn't be accepted! There must be a queue of girls waiting for such a chance.'

'There is! But he knows someone there — he'll wrangle and cajole — ' Michael's mother sat down as if she needed to sit. 'And won't it be marvellous? Mind you — he liked Judy, the girl in hospital — a lovely dancer, but he really dislikes Jessie Jenkins — not exactly in a personal way, you know. But as his dancing partner, she's just not on! Ah, here he is! Michael — I've been breaking the news as gently as I could.'

'Good! So you are on television tonight, Debbie! Eat a good meal now, because you are going to work hard! Pile up her plate, mother — give her plenty!'

'Well — you can see, I'm doing just that!'

'Michael — Mrs. Thornton — ' breathlessly, Debbie spooned half the delicious chicken and mushroom from her plate. 'I couldn't possibly — '

'I'll put on a record and we'll rehearse in the other room! We're not on till eight o'clock. Loads of time! Heaven sent!'

The next hour was strenuous, to say the least of it, but for Debbie a strangely unexpected tension-releasing, curiously satisfying experience. She laughed a lot and — as often happened when she danced — cried a little, making no apology for her tears, nor explaining them, nor was she asked to do so. Michael simply put his arm round her shoulder, murmuring something like, 'There — there — things work out. Nothing lasts. You think you're at the end of your tether. Then you open another lucky bag! Eh? That's life. Come, on, let's run through that number again.'

'Am I doing all right, Michael? I mean — I've never danced on television in my life.'

'Not to worry. You don't have to worry. You've got what it takes! Born for it! Born for it!'

The show took place in a converted barn a few miles from the city centre, somewhere in the region of the Dublin mountains. Michael had no car of his own, but he hired one, and they turned off a main road at a sign-post, pointing to 'Sallynoggin'.

'They hold Art exhibitions and Craft shows and all sorts of things in this joint. Tonight, it's a Pop Dance in a Pub, for television. My big chance, really, because I happen to know there's someone special coming — big shot in show business!'

They found the barn, after a couple of wrong turnings. It was an authentic old barn with rough walls and ancient beams, and the atmosphere when they entered was blue with smoke, crowded, and very noisy. A television unit was being fitted up, and someone was warning that soon the crowd would have to go and the air cleared. Michael introduced Debbie to a big man with fierce, dark eyes and a lot of black beard, so that one saw little else of his face. He looked at her, doubtfully, in silence.

'I warned you not to judge by the outside, didn't I?' Michael exclaimed, as though Debbie were not there.

'You did — but this is not what we want — '

'Give us a chance, eh?'

'It's your funeral, Mike! You know who's to be here tonight. And Jessie raised hell, and she's gone off in a blue blaze, and it's more than likely we're in for a law case.'

'Rot! We signed nothing! Anyway, I told you I can't dance with her!'

'Yes, but she won't take that. Look Mike — let me phone her back, for God's sake. This — this is not the type.' He indicated Debbie, in much the same way as he might indicate a piece of furniture.

'I tell you she's *it*! Look — if I'm wrong, I lose everything? Contract, everything?'

'O.K.' The big man shrugged, then went away to a group of electricians, and took no further notice of Michael or his new partner-to-be.

'You'll have to get dressed, and some make-up on!' Michael gently urged the girl on before him towards the dressing-rooms. 'Yellow stuff, but it comes out all right in the picture.'

Debbie found herself in a brightly lit room where several large mirrors hung on rough walls, and in which she saw herself and other girls reflected scores of times, dimming off into confused distance. Presently, I'll wake up, she thought in a sort of daze. This can't be real! I have to be at the hospital at nine in the morning.

Someone was holding a red dress up against her. 'It's too small. You're much bigger than Miss Jenkins, Miss!'

Michael was waiting in the doorway. 'That's your job, Mary! *Make* it fit, and be smart about it! She's on at eight, sharp!' He smiled, coming back into the room for a moment to put a firm hand on Debbie's shoulder. 'You're Tops! Keep that in mind! Be seein' you.'

'Well, Miss, I ask you!' The dresser stared after him. 'He's the limit, so he is! This is far too tight in the bust — '

'Let me try!' Debbie removed her tunic and 'mini', no longer heeding the people about her. The dressing room and the people in it, and everything happening just then must be regarded as a sort of dream. But she'd do her best. In an unreal sort of way she was enjoying every moment, and this girl Mary, was worried about the dress.

'I'm pretty clever at altering things,' Debbie confided, slipping the dress over her head. 'Now — have you a pair of scissors? Needle and thread? Plenty of letting out here.'

'Oh, thank you, Miss. What a relief!' Mary smiled, found what was required, and a comparatively quiet corner to work in. Debbie snipped and pulled, slipped in and out of the dress, put in some firm stitches, twirled about in front of a long mirror, and enquired, triumphantly — 'How's that?'

'Lovely! Looks better on you than on the other young lady. She's too fair for this shade of red, really. 'Course it's coloured telly! Very special — otherwise it wouldn't matter much.'

'Well now for this queer make-up!'

'Oh, I'm used to that — but when it's for coloured TV it's like stage make-up, really. Just sit here, Miss, and we'll soon have you right. Tonight's special. That's why it's coloured.'

Debbie relaxed in her chair, closing her eyes, and giving herself up to the

216

make-up girl, completely. She found Mary's cool fingers soothing. She thought with confidence of what lay before her. She believed she would be successful, because she knew exactly what Michael wanted. They fitted each other like hand in glove, Michael and she, dancing. She was no longer nervous nor even anxious. She would do exactly as he had indicated, exactly as he wanted, and she would enjoy every moment of it, because every moment of all this unexpected experience was blotting out, for the time being, the pain and the aching misery waiting behind a closed door in her mind and heart. Later on, she'd have to deal with the misery and the ache. But now she would dance, dance, dance with Michael. It didn't matter if it were on television or in an empty room. Nothing mattered except the movement, the rhythm, and the music. She was almost asleep when Mary removed the nylon protecting cover. 'Now, Miss, you're ready.'

She had not long to wait for Michael, and they went on into the barn. The scene had changed. The air was fresh and clear of smoke, the crowd had gone. Only a few tables were on the floor with selected people sitting drinking beer from tankards. Others were waiting for the signal to begin dancing. A band was in place on a rostrum. Other dancers stood expectantly, smiling, under the brightest possible lights. The floor was clear and shining. Great jars of colourful flowers banked the band-stand. The actor 'bar-man' in white coat, behind a cocktail bar, was shaking a cocktail. Debbie could hear the ice jingling. Then, someone shouted an order, dropped an arm, and at once the scene came to life. The band started and dancing began. People at the tables chatted as naturally as if there were no cameras focused on them, and a waiter went, casually, about the tables, filling tankards, selling cigarettes and chocolate.

Suddenly, Michael was coming across

the floor, his arms extended towards Debbie, the familiar twinkle in his blue eyes. She saw how his thick red hair shone like gold under the lights, how jaunty he looked as he came confidently, gaily, towards her, and then they were off!

It was exhilarating! It was heavenly! Debbie danced as she had never danced before. At times, it seemed to her, she was scarcely touching the floor. In and out under Michael's arms she moved, light as thistledown. She was switched, wafted, lifted, set down, twirled about like an autumn leaf. She loved it.

But, in no time at all, it seemed, it was over! No — there was tremendous clapping and cries for more. And they were off again. This time, Michael had only time to make a quick sign to the band leader, and to whisper — 'Same as we did back at the colonel's party! Follow!' Debbie found herself being led and enticed and challenged, and for a while she forgot everything in the world except the dance, the music, the joining in of other dancers, the clapping, the laughter, and the sudden ending.

It was really over. Another group was coming on to sing ballads and strum guitars, and Michael was leading her away from the scene into another room where a supper table was laid. The big black-bearded man was there, standing with his back to the long stone mantelpiece. His expression now, however, was no longer fierce or slightly contemptuous, but smiling, showing very white teeth.

'I owe you an apology, Miss Holden. You're It! You don't look the type, but as Mike asserted, you're *It*! Sit down. We're having supper in a few moments.'

Some other girls and young men came to join them at the table. Everyone seemed to be on terms, seemed to know each other, relaxed and happy, with that particular glow about them to be observed by show people, after a good performance. One of the girls sitting next to Debbie said

— 'You're new? You really are marvellous! We all are agreed on that! Have some of this cold roast beef and salad. Gosh — I'm starving. I'm sure you are, too.' She heaped Debbie's plate, not waiting for an answer.

A little breathlessly, still, the newcomer agreed that she was extremely hungry, and that she had never danced on television before.

'Well, take it from me, you'll be on TV again! You're a fantastic dancer.'

Someone on the opposite side of the table exclaimed — 'Judy may look out!'

Debbie was enjoying her meal, and was not greatly interested in Judy. She wasn't ever going to get in Judy's way. Someone had filled her glass with a fragrant rose wine, and she was ravenously hungry. The big man with the black beard had been talking a lot to Michael, and when the meal was over, both he and Michael came across to her.

'I'd like to see some more of your

dancing, Miss Holden. A 'Very Important Person' was here during your turn, and he is impressed! You've certainly got what it takes!'

Michael sat down beside her, hugging her, exuberantly. 'Debbie — we are made! I knew how it would be — right from the first moment I saw you dance back there in the West. You're going to be offered a job as my dancing partner — permanent! Smallish payment to begin with, perhaps, but rising to heaven knows where, in a short while! Gee — you must have been born under a lucky star!'

'Not so fast there, Mike! I never said anything about her signing on, as your exclusive partner! You're fine together, sure, but all sorts of things might arise, or she may go solo, or with a group, or any way we wish! Got that!'

'O.K., Hitler!'

'Yes. But *I* haven't quite 'got it',' Debbie interpolated, looking, coolly, from one to the other. 'I came here this evening to help Michael out. I've loved every moment of it. But I'm signing no contract to dance on TV. My job's nursing. I'm just a plain hospital nurse.'

'Take that, Big Boss!' Michael grinned, sitting on the edge of the table swinging his legs. 'But, of course, she doesn't mean a word of it. She's not altogether insane!'

'No — I'm reasonably sane, I hope.' Debbie smiled at the two faces, one astounded, the other amused and unbelieving.

'Phew! Well, I suppose I deserved that!' The big man strode over to the mantelpiece again, displeased. 'What the hell did you mean by misleading me, then, Mike. Wasting time.' He glared at the unconcerned girl.

'This is an awful 'let-down' for him, Debbie! He can't take it in, that anyone could possibly say 'No' to the great man! Scores of girls lined up — waiting for a small chance — even in a crowd, and you calmly turn down the chance in a million! Or *seem* to — clever girl!

But you aren't really turning this down!'

The door swung open. The black-bearded man put up his hand for silence. 'Who the hell — Why isn't it locked as usual?'

They were looking into the barn where transmission on the next part of the programme was just starting. The studio manager signalled 'Vision On', then 'Sound On', dropping his arm for the action to start. Someone slipped quickly over to the door and closed and locked it.

'Can't we get out, now?' Debbie enquired when the faces round her became relaxed again.

'Course we can — there's the street, or the road door,' Michael indicated a great door on the opposite side of the room. 'Can't imagine how the studio door wasn't locked.'

'Are you refusing my offer, Miss Holden?' the big man inquired, sitting down to his supper, and when she said simply — 'Thank you. It's a great privilege, and someone else will soon jump at such an offer, but I am not in a position to accept.'

After that, the man poured himself a glass of wine and turning away from Debbie and Michael, chatted with the young people on the opposite side of the table, completely losing interest.

'You can't be serious?' Michael blazed. 'Debbie Holden, you're mad.'

'Maybe. But I've never been more serious in my life. I don't want to be a TV star.' She stood up. 'I'm really sorry to disappoint you, all the same, Michael. But you've already got a perfect partner. What about Judy?'

'Oh, don't bother me about Judy. She's a good dancer, and we do get along, but not the way you and I do. Joe had plans for promotion for her, too, if you had taken her place.'

'Who's Joe?'

'His Lordship! Sitting with his back to you!' Michael indicated the big man. 'Look — take a day or two, to consider it? I believe we've rushed you off your feet? You're bewildered. Tired. Not prepared!'

Joe turned slowly round. 'Will you stop being a nuisance, and take the girl home to bed!' There was a roar of good-natured laughter from the supper crowd.

'I'm in no humour for your smart alec jokes, either!' Infuriated, Michael escorted Debbie out of the supper-room, with a brief wave of 'Goodnight', intended to include everybody. When they got the car started, he sat in silence beside his worried companion for some minutes.

'Don't be vexed, Michael,' she said, gently. 'I hope we will often dance together and have lots of fun. Only — not on television or in professional partnership.'

'Debbie Holden, you've let me down badly! You're not sane. No one on earth would have turned down such a chance.'

'Don't be silly! Lots would!'

'O.K. Let's leave it, Nursie!' Michael's headlights frightened a cat crossing the road out of its wits so that the poor animal landed up into the branches of a tree.

'You nearly killed it! You're so cross and bad-tempered. I shall certainly have no regrets about not being in partnership with you! Gosh — you've got a frightful temper! Red hair, I suppose.' She laughed, suddenly, or rather, giggled, helplessly, for the moment, almost enjoying Michael's understandable annoyance and finding herself in an unaccountable mood for teasing.

He slowed down and stopped, turning to gaze at her averted face. 'Don't worry — I'm not going to make any passes at you — just trying to make you out!'

'Indeed?' She smiled, turning back to meet his scrutiny in the dim light. 'You shouldn't have much trouble! I'm a terribly ordinary sort. They turn me out by the million!'

'I wonder? Now, who — in her proper senses — would coolly turn down Fame and Fortune! We'll say nothing about what you've done to me!'

'You've said quite enough about that! Besides, you ought to have some regard for Judy. *Men*!' Debbie's head lifted in contempt, her dark eyes sultry with a returning wave of personal misery. 'All the same! Bone selfish!'

He was silent, staring at the road. 'Well — maybe I'm a bit of a cad! Trying to force fame and fortune on a nice, but unwilling girl, nursing her own private heart-break, as well as people in hospital! Let's say 'PAX' and be done with it, eh? But my God — it's a fierce disappointment. I'll get you to your digs. You have to be at that old depot in the morning at the damned crack of dawn!' He started the car and shot forward down the white winding road.

'It's not an old depot. It's probably the best hospital in the whole of Ireland! And nine o'clock isn't the 'crack of dawn'. It's the normal, reasonable, right time for everybody to be up and about, unless they're sick!'

'I must be terribly sick, so!'

'In a way, you are! Anybody not able to face the everyday little ups and downs of life — must be sick!'

'Not even sorry for me, eh? No little sedative?' Outside the hall door of her digs, he slid an arm back of her seat.

'It's a prick in the arm you want — a good lively shot — not a sedative, Michael Thornton!' She made to get out of the car.

'I say, Debbie — let's not part this way? Let's be real friends?' He brushed a butterfly kiss against her ear, and moved back to the wheel. 'For God's sake, don't drop me.'

'I haven't the slightest intention of dropping you, darling Mike!' She laughed, out on the pavement, searching for the key she had been given.

'Could you possibly remain on — say for two nights a week, until Judy's better? Could you do *that* much?'

She hesitated. 'Well, then, yes, I'll do that, if it's a help, but I've got to get back to the hospital early, remember, and the bit of 'help' must not interfere with my working hours.'

'I'll see it won't. That's a promise. Thank you for that crumb of kind consolation! Night! Sleep well.'

He was gone, and Debbie put the key in the door, too exhausted for further thought or speculation, sleeping like a log, the moment her tired, brown-haired head reached the pillow.

11

Back at Abbey Farm, Dermot Gregory
came downstairs at the usual time on
the morning after his experience at
Penrose House. It was his custom to
brew a mug of strong tea before going
out-of-doors, since Mrs. Ramsay and
breakfast would not be available until
somewhat later. At the foot of the stairs
he glanced at the hall table where he
noticed an envelope, and absent-
mindedly, wondering at such a small
and early postal arrival, he picked up
the envelope to discover that it had
been left there by Debbie. It was
addressed to his mother, in Debbie's
handwriting. Puzzled, he put it back
where he found it, and thought no
more about it until some hours later,
after some delay in the sheds, he came
into the breakfast room to find his
mother with tear-filled eyes. 'Here he is

231

now, Mrs. Ramsay — sorry you have to start breakfast all over again, but things are not normal anywhere, this morning.' He saw Debbie's letter open on the table.

Mrs. Ramsay, looking grim, murmured something about bacon and eggs and left the room.

'What's to do, Ma?' Dermot inquired, concerned.

'Debbie's gone! She's left us!' Mrs. Gregory exclaimed, picking up the single sheet of notepaper and handing it to him.

'Gone? She can't be gone. Is this hers?'

'Yes. She put it on the hall table for me — last night, it would seem, before she slipped out of the house. You may read it. Indeed, there's nothing in it which doesn't apply to us both. What on earth are we going to do without her?'

He read the short note in silence. It was merely to say that Debbie hated 'goodbyes', but that she felt the time had come for a change, and after a while she hoped to come back to see Mrs. Gregory and darling Mark who wouldn't miss her for long, since he would soon start school. The short letter ended with a word of thanks for 'five wonderful years as one of the Gregory family' and wishing loads of luck to Abbey Farm.

'Silly girl!' Dermot threw the letter on the table, impatiently. 'Fancy writing, instead of coming straight to tell us she was in need of a change. Not a bit like her.' He sat down at the table as Mrs. Ramsay brought in a pot of coffee with some bacon and eggs.

When they were alone again, he exclaimed, impatiently — 'For heaven's sake, stop crying, Ma! It's not the end of the world.'

'No — ' Mrs. Gregory blew her nose, putting the letter back into its envelope with an air of resolution. 'No — it's not the end of the world, but it's going to be a different house without Debbie — that's all. Mark is impossible to handle this morning. Mrs. Ramsay has been in and out, asking questions about his clothes and about what to say to him. He keeps on asking questions, of course, and wanting to run off out because he thinks Debbie is hiding somewhere outside.'

'You'll have to get busy on all that, Mother dear!'

Galvanised into activity by Dermot's apparent casual acceptance of the situation, his mother went away to deal with the problem of Mark and his clothes. The latter she found in perfect order, folded and mended and laundered to the smallest, least important article. She busied herself taking stock of everything and consoling the little boy. 'Oh, I'm sure she'll be back in a few days,' she said lightly. 'She's just gone for a little holiday because she was tired — that's all.' In consoling the child with such wishful thinking, she began to cheer herself. Perhaps this hopeful attitude was the right one. It was not so much the loss of a hitherto indispensable companion who had become as dear to her as a daughter, which caused Mrs. Gregory's tears but the putting away of a dream, the abandonment of her dearest hope.

Dermot's seeming careless acceptance of the girl's departure had not only stopped her tears and galvanised her into action, but it had shocked her into further surprise and the beginning of speculation about Debbie's departure. Was Dermot as cold and ungrateful, and so unperturbed as to seem unfeeling towards the girl who had done so much for him? He used not to be like this. What had happened to change him? Meriel? Was Meriel the root cause of Debbie's departure? Mrs. Gregory stood in the middle of the nursery floor holding a pile of newly-laundered pullovers. It was as though an electric light had been switched on in her mind. She answered Mark's innumerable questions automatically, and for the rest of that day found herself so preoccupied and so busy that there was, literally, no time for the sadness which had first enveloped her, on reading Debbie's letter that morning. Sources of energy lying dormant, were called upon, and instead of sitting about, brooding on her loss and on the fear of what might be coming to change everything, including herself and Dermot at Abbey Farm, she found that she was giving her best self to her troubled grandson, and finding consolation — even a new source of joy — in so doing. Then, there were all the household concerns — the division of unaccustomed chores between herself and Mrs. Ramsay.

In the evening, when Dermot appeared for supper after his shower and change of clothing, he found his mother a surprisingly more cheerful person than he had dared to expect. Yet she could not abandon the subject uppermost in her mind. She had decided that it was best to talk openly as opportunity and inclination dictated — to keep things as casual and spontaneous as possible. She wanted no brooding silences between herself and her son. She was determined, gradually and without seeming tension, to discover just what was in his mind concerning both Debbie and Meriel Dean.

'You know, my dear, I've quite made up my mind about all this change of things,' she announced, towards the end of the meal. 'It's going to be hard at first — missing dear Deb. But I'm quite resolved to face up to it sensibly. We mustn't be selfish. She wanted to get her diploma — I've always known that. And in a few weeks, I hope to have overcome my sadness at her departure and got myself so well in hand, that I shall take a trip to Dublin to see her because, you know, I'm simply refusing to break with Debbie. It's unthinkable.'

'Very sensible. Exactly what I had intended advising you to do.' He paused. 'And do remember, mother, that you and Mark are not the only two who will miss her.'

She glanced at him quickly. 'You will

— miss her — too? But, of course, you will!'

'Yes, I'll miss her. Especially as I found the cheque we have all been looking for, arrived in this morning's post!' He stood with his back to the fireplace. 'So we must get down to a lot of planning, and the all-important advisability of making Walter an offer for the Long Meadows and the fields up at Knockadee — poor Debbie's great preoccupation — ' he concluded, as though the thought had just occurred to him. 'Remember how she used to keep on about them?'

'You got the cheque! And you do not mention it — even — till now!' Mrs. Gregory was torn between joy in the arrival, at last, of real money which was going to make such a difference in their lives, and a sense of wild irritation with her son for not having told her such good news the very moment he had received the solicitor's letter, which he now handed over to her.

'But why didn't you tell me at once!

Dermot, you can be quite exasperating, you really can! Why wait till this time of evening to let me have this good news?'

He did not answer immediately. 'I suppose I should have done that. But I only got round to opening my letters just before supper! Then — well — it took some time to register the fact! You know I had a sort of superstitious fear that it was all nonsense about the picture, and that we would soon be told that. I can hardly believe that such luck can possibly come my way — all that money — out of the blue, so to speak!'

'It's not a bit 'out of the blue'. It's just payment for a famous work of art which belonged to your family for generations!' his mother exclaimed, indignantly. 'Indeed, I'm only sorry that it had to go out of the family, at all — but what could we do, wanting the money so badly.'

'And then I kept thinking that but only for Debbie, our picture might still be hanging here in its panel over my head — with the same old grind of near-poverty obstructing every hope for improvement — '

As he spoke, thoughtfully filling a pipe, hardly realising that he spoke his thoughts aloud, his mother saw with glad surprise, that the mask of outer casualness, that maddening casualness, which had so distressed her, was, in reality, the mask of a very serious and sober young man, with something of big import growing in his mind.

Having worked and slept and got back into routine, he was reviewing the events of the past few days with calmer, more normal judgement. The fact of his one lapse into drunkenness did not unduly distress him. That had been a mere blow to his pride, a bad mistake on his part, for personal and family reasons. It was something which would not occur again. He had made a fool of himself. Face it. No point in blaming Meriel, either. Had he been half a man, he told himself, bitterly, her contrivings and her jibes would have had no effect. He recalled the session in the garden of the hotel with horror. He had made love to a beautiful 'vixen' of a young woman for whom he had no particle of affection. No matter if she had made all the advances at first. He had made love to her — he had called her back and tried to keep her there — The thing, now, was to let her know, as decently as possible, that such love-making meant nothing. He had guessed Debbie was gone after the meeting on the stairs, and in the hallway the following morning. Strange, he mused, how small an effect this seemed to have on him at the time. It was as though some mental iron curtain had descended between him and the fact that she had gone.

During the next few days, however, this numbed condition of mind gradually changed to a sense of depression and even of desolation. At every turn he missed the girl with the great trusting brown eyes, the winning smile, the sensible 'down-to-earth' attitude towards life and people. He missed that helpful, willing hand, as ready to be useful in the stable yard or the fields, as in the house. His mother had been shaken into activity and was coping with the situation not very successfully. Mark was fretful and unmanagable.

'I'm afraid you will have to take a firmer hand with him, Dermot,' Mrs. Gregory insisted, one evening, a few days after Debbie's departure. 'He is fine, for a while, every day. Then he begins those tearful questions — it's heart-breaking, really. I can't seem to control him at times.'

Dermot did not like to see those tired lines under his mother's eyes. But the fact had the effect of making him even more bad-tempered than he already felt. 'O.K. I'll take him in hand a bit more. Did you write to the hospital?' he enquired, abruptly.

'Of course, I did. And I mentioned that you had got your cheque, and that you had applied for the Long Acre fields.'

'No reply, so far?'

'Indeed, no. Even though I asked her

what I was to do with the suit cases left in her room. But if I had a reply you may be sure I would tell you, immediately,' his mother declared with some asperity.

'Don't nag, Ma! Something you never used to do.'

'Sorry!' Hurt, his mother left the room to fetch the tea tray. But returned looking more composed. 'It's true, Dermot. I've been as cross as sticks most of the time, lately — since Debbie left. I've tried — but, so far, I don't seem able to take it.'

'She's entitled to a life of her own. We've been very possessive about her.'

'But she seemed so happy here — '

'She has chosen to leave.'

'I wonder why?' Mrs. Gregory looked searchingly into her son's face, but the face told her nothing. The expression there was hard and cold and remote. She realised with a strange certainty, that Dermot was more involved than he was willing to admit. She would have to be patient. She would have to wait.

They were interrupted by the phone ringing in the hall. Dermot was not surprised to hear Meriel's voice at the other end.

'Goodness! You are hard to get!' she laughingly accused. 'This is the third time of asking. Have you forgotten — you promised to come and help me decide about that colt over at Frazers'? Do try and find time to come over tomorrow afternoon?'

'Meriel, I've already told you that I have no time at all for such diversions! But, since I am deeply indebted to you for all you've done for Big Boy, I will *make* time to drop over in the late afternoon, tomorrow, although your own judgement in such matters is as good — probably far ahead of mine.'

'Nonsense, Mr. Modest!'

'Er — by-the-way — I did want to have a chat with you, Meriel,' he went on. 'So we can kill two birds with the one stone, so to speak!'

'You sound sort of 'narked', not to say mysterious!' she accused.

'Do I? Sorry about that. I shouldn't sound 'narked' to someone who has done so much for me. Have you heard anything from Tomlin, since, I mean, about that horse of mine?'

'He was talking to daddy on the phone last night. I assure you he is well and truly sold — to Big Boy. Daddy says Noble is going to be beaten! But whether he is, or not, you're in luck, Dermot.'

'Well — admitted! I held on to him when I couldn't afford him because I felt he had what it takes!'

'Oh, I say,' she ran on, lightly, 'is it true you have lost your valuable Nurse Holden? Extraordinary how things get around. I heard it, today, in the new supermarket, of all places!'

'Quite a likely place for gossip! But I wouldn't say we have 'lost' her! She's away for a while. She'll be back.' He heard himself make the statement very firmly, albeit lightly and even casually — 'she'll be back.'

'Indeed?' There was a little pause. 'I

heard she had gone for good, up to town to hospital nursing, again.'

'Gossip!'

'Of course. But that's life in a small town, isn't it. Anyway, your little boy is growing up, now. Didn't you tell us he will be starting Prep school in the autumn? He's beyond the 'Nannie' stage!'

'True! Mark's quite a fellow.' Dermot did not amend what his heart was saying about his little boy — 'only crying out for her, most of the day, since she left.'

He pulled up his wandering thoughts. Meriel was still talking. 'None the worse for our party the other night?' she enquired gaily.

'Oh, not a bit! Considerably the better, in fact, Meriel! I hope your father and you were not exhausted after all that junketing!'

'Daddy confessed to feeling a bit dopy the next day. But he thoroughly enjoyed it.'

'Fine! Be seeing you round four

o'clock, tomorrow.'

'Lovely!' They hung up, Dermot with a rather set line about his mouth. This was something he had to do, and the sooner it was done, the better.

Already, a long-coveted man had been hired for the farm, and it was with an easy conscience, though with intense reluctance that Dermot set out for Rockinish and Penrose House, the next afternoon. Colonel Penrose met him on the steps, delighted to see him and clearly anxious to talk, but Dermot explained, hastily, the reason for his visit.

'I understand, dear boy! Meriel is out in the stable yard waiting for you. The Frazers are selling their colt. Meriel fancies it — so do I, in fact, but she relies greatly on your judgement.'

'Her own is pretty sound, sir — not to mention yours!'

'Well,' he laughed, 'there it is, Dermot. My girl is bent on having your advice in the matter! How is your mother? I hear you have lost your invaluable little help — Miss Holden. Too bad.'

'We haven't 'lost' Debbie, exactly, Colonel. She's — er — she's nursing for a while, in order to obtain some diploma or other. She'll be back.'

'Will she?' The older man looked at him, curiously. Then went on in his usual 'hearty' way — 'Mrs. Gregory and you must come along some evening, soon, and have a nice, leisurely dinner? Perhaps one evening next week?'

'Thank you, Colonel. But you had better talk to my mother about that. I expect she'd be pleased.'

'We all feel she doesn't get about nearly enough — we are intending to change all that!'

Dermot escaped round to the back of the house, to find Meriel chatting with a stable-boy. She turned to greet him with a certain conscious look in her beautiful blue eyes. They were narrowed a little as she scrutinised his face. The more she saw of Dermot Gregory, the more attracted she became. His love-making on the night of their 'little dinner' for two, had been, for her, an unexpectedly thrilling experience. There had been a fiery reality in Dermot's kiss — a demand — which had left her in thrall, and for the first time in her somewhat amorous, adventurous life, she was in the power of a young man, obsessed by desire for him, and wildly determined to get what she wanted. But she was also determined that this must be no casual 'affair'. Marriage with this up and coming young farmer, whose life and farming she would soon mould to her liking, was her object — the reason for her hurried exit from the hotel garden. This was, she told herself, caught in the web of her own spinning, 'the real thing'.

'If you're sure you really want my opinion — ' Dermot began.

'But I do. Most decidedly!'

'I see. Well, hop in here into the old Austin, so, if you don't too much object to her age and somewhat draughty interior, and we'll run across to Frazers'.'

'Fine! And don't be silly about the old car, Dermot! You'll soon buy a super one, and be the envy of the neighbourhood!' She slipped into the seat beside him, her shoulder touching his, in a sort of caress.

The now familiar slight fragrance of her perfume assailed his senses, as on previous occasions. But this time, however, he was prepared. He admitted her allure, and could not but acknowledge with a certain native humility, that it was no small privilege to be liked by such a wonderful young woman. Were he free —. Thoughtfully, he pulled himself up. Puzzled, he became silent as they drove along the twisting roadway with its dense green hedges, starred with honeysuckle and the last of the wild roses. Was he not entirely free? Free as air? Why should he not, at least, try to meet the girl's advances in the expected way. He knew her faults — he could not trust her — even her kindness about his horse was, he felt, not disinterested. He had been aware of it from the beginning. She wanted something from him. Why could he not respond? Why had a question about his freedom come into his mind? To whom, or to what was he 'bound'?

'Penny for them! You look as though you were solving the riddle of the universe!' she laughed.

'Maybe I am, at that!' he grinned. 'We turn left, here, I think.'

'That's it. Honeysuckle — wild strawberries — wild roses — isn't it a magical time of the year! I'm so glad you were able to come along this afternoon, Dermot — I mean, that you are getting some of the help at the Abbey Farm you so badly need.'

'I've often wanted to get hold of Tim Burke — splendid fellow — worth every penny, now, of the biggish wages I have to fork out!'

'Splendid! And you'll go on expanding? Daddy tells me you are buying land all round you like a good 'un!'

'Your dad is exaggerating. No offence. But I'm not buying land like that, indeed.'

'Those Long Acre fields — I happen to know — '

'Oh, yes. I've got those back all right. They belonged in the family for generations.'

'Tell me about them — and about what else you have in mind regarding land?' she requested, eagerly.

Oddly reluctant to talk about his plans — even somewhat resentful at being questioned, he pretended a sudden interest in a cottage which was being colour-washed, avoiding any answer. He had no intention of discussing his farm with Meriel Dean. She did not belong in that part of his life. That was it — she didn't *belong*. He pushed the idea into the back of his mind, and humoured her by a superficial joining in her gay mood, until they pulled up at Frazers', and found their way over to the paddocks where the owner of the colt met them.

An hour or so passed very pleasantly,

and Dermot found himself genuinely involved in horses, and in the colt, in particular — a sprightly, spirited little animal, rather small, perhaps, but eminently suitable for Meriel's riding school requirements. Meriel was at her best in such circumstances, and the business of the afternoon was concluded by her purchase of the horse and accepting a drink in the house to 'clinch' the deal.

Dermot waited outside in the car, and when Meriel joined him, as she did in a very short time, she was pouting a little. 'You really ought to have come in! How horrid of you!'

'Your going in was sufficient for the social side, Meriel! Frazer knows me long and well enough to understand and condone my 'uncivilised' behaviour! Or, at least, what *you* would consider 'uncivilised'!'

She saw that it would be a mistake to comment further, and anxious to keep him for supper at home, she ran on, eagerly, 'You gave me just that bit of extra confidence! Even my father has made mistakes, you know — bad mistakes. But I don't think you could ever go wrong about a horse, Dermot?'

'Sheer flattery, Meriel! No one on earth is infallible where horses are concerned!'

When they reached Penrose House and the main street of Rockinish, Dermot politely opened the door for Meriel, but in doing so, hesitated. There was something he must say to her and now was the time.

'But, you'll come in and join us at our evening meal, surely?' Meriel ignored the open car door and remained seated where she was.

'You must excuse me — ' he glanced at his watch. 'I've got to get back. Must!'

'Oh, but what was it you so mysteriously wanted to say to me? I've been waiting all afternoon to know!'

'Yes — well, it's just something which ought to have been said long before this — ' he began.

But Meriel smilingly stopped the car engine. 'Come on! We can't possibly talk here in the middle of the traffic. Besides, my father has the door open. Look — he's expecting you to come in.'

Dermot saw that this was so. And perhaps what he had to say was better said in the privacy of the house. He followed the young woman up the steps and into the spacious library where Colonel Penrose indicated a comfortable armchair.

'Meriel has just told me — she's bought the horse! On her way into the kitchen! You're staying for a bit of supper with us?'

There was nothing for it but to agree, and the young man dropped casually into the armchair, very much wishing he were not there, although nothing could be more welcoming or friendly than the colonel. But Dermot dreaded any further intimacy, and was greatly relieved when his host was called to answer the phone. This intimate supper 'get-together' was something Dermot had urgently hoped to avoid. He flicked over the pages of a sporting magazine, impatiently, wishing that what he had to say to Meriel could be said quickly and without fuss, and that he could escape without joining in the evening meal.

Suddenly, the door opened and Meriel ran into the room and over to a television set, switching on in a most agitated manner. 'It's on in the kitchen — Katey called my attention to it. You simply won't believe your eyes,' she exclaimed. 'Just look!'

He threw down the magazine and looked across the room at the television set, and there, to his utter amazement, he found himself looking at Debbie Holden. The screen was showing a close-up of her face, at that moment. The great dark eyes were calmly gazing out under the familiar fringe of straight hair. She was being enthusiastically applauded by the studio audience, after dancing. Then the bearded young man came into view beside her, and they were off again, into a whirl of intricate,

seemingly abandoned, yet very con-
trolled movement. Dermot's eyes were
riveted on the screen, following the
convolutions of the two. He already
knew something of what Debbie was
capable of in the sphere of pop
dancing, of her strange, unexpected
emergence at times into the realm of
ballet, so light and graceful that her
rather square body became trans-
formed. Presenting a swan-like poetic
beauty — something more of the mind
than the body. But he had never seen
anything like this before. It was
extraordinarily good. It seemed to him
as though he looked at some inspired
aspect of Debbie which was new and
exciting and very troubling. He did not
know how long the dancing went on
until he became aware of Meriel's
voice, harsh and grating on his ears.

'So! There's your 'good-goody' hospital nurse! There's your so solid,
demure, reticent little Nurse Holden!
We do live and learn, don't we!'

Jealousy had taken possession of

Meriel, in much the same way as that passion had consumed her years ago when Dermot married Ann. Once again, although in a different way, he was absorbed to the exclusion of everything but the girl dancing on television. When Meriel spoke, she saw the look in his grey eyes. She had thought to shock him, but her effort had the opposite effect. Yet, she ran on, unable to stop herself — 'What a deceitful piece she must be — to put all this over on you! Hospital nursing, indeed!'

Dermot stood up when the programme changed. Meriel switched off. There was a tense silence in the room between them.

'Don't you agree?' Meriel demanded.

'I do not agree. I couldn't disagree more. Debbie Holden is incapable of deceit.'

'What utter nonsense! Don't you even see that that programme is a repeat? She must have been on some days ago — immediately after leaving your farm! But I observe you are such a champion you can't see straight!'

'I don't like the tone of your voice, Meriel. I don't like your attitude. Debbie was — and still is — a member of my family to whom we are most deeply indebted. She is my mother's friend, my son's foster mother — '

'And your — sister!' Meriel threw back her head in a shrill laugh of mockery. 'Jolly good joke, that!'

'It would be more accurate to call her my very dear and valued friend. To her I owe the life of Mark, and my mother's recovery from an extremely grave illness.'

Making a supreme effort, Meriel changed her tactics. 'I'm sorry, Dermot. I didn't realise all this — I wouldn't offend you for the earth. You see — I thought this girl was merely a sort of paid house help — and that she was deliberately deceiving you and Mrs. Gregory.'

'She is a professional nurse, who left aside the final stage of her hospital training in order to assist us at the Abbey Farm, at our earnest request, almost six years ago.'

'But surely she must be playing some double game, now? I know Michael Thornton — he was at our house-warming party. He is a friend of Dr. Kelly's, a law student. But I did hear he had signed some sort of contract to dance on television. He must have been working very hard for some time to get her into that racket, and she must have known quite well what she was intending to do when she left you so suddenly. You *must* see that much, Dermot? You have now witnessed with your own eyes she is not in nursing. But — forgive me, my dear.' Meriel in her accustomed impulsive way, slipped her arm into Dermot's. 'I don't mean to be horrid. But I do hate to see you, and your mother — such a sweet trusting creature as she is — so blatantly deceived. Come — let's go and join daddy. Supper's ready. I'm sorry I turned on that wretched TV.'

'Before we leave, Meriel,' Dermot gently withdrew the possessive arm, and walked to the other side of the room, standing with his back to the window. 'Let me say that I don't know what's happened about this dancing, but I do know that Debbie Holden is incapable of deceit. I am absolutely certain that she has not deliberately misled us.'

Meriel shrugged. 'Oh, well — '

'Just a moment more, and I'm done,' he smiled a little apologetically. 'I wanted to — er — to apologise to you, Meriel, for what happened in the hotel garden the other night — '

She laughed, elegant eyebrows raised, intrigued. 'Why — because of your getting 'blotto'? Oh, you were funny, Dermot darling!'

'That, too. But it was what happened afterwards.'

'Oh — I see. I understand! You dear impossible old stupid! That was nothing! Fun! And — ' She stepped across the room to stand near him. 'I liked it!'

'It wasn't 'fun' — to me. I took

advantage of you, Meriel — and I really do apologise — ' Unable to explain himself, he turned abruptly to look unseeingly out of the curtained window.

'Well — you blessed old Victorian!' She laughed her little mocking amused laugh. But something about the set of his shoulders stopped her at that moment from any further attempt at the intimacy she craved. Instead, she opened the door. 'Come along — it's mushrooms and things! You'll love them. And — please — do not make mountains out of molehills, you odd creature. After all, you and I are not 'teenagers'. We're adult! At least — I am!'

'Well — that's that.' He turned back into the room. 'I'm afraid I mustn't stay — I really must go. I'm so glad you've got your fine little colt.'

'How horrid of you not to stay — '

But no pleading or pouting or cajoling had any effect. Hot under the collar, angry, embarrassed, and worried beyond any pretence at conviviality, he found himself, at last, driving as fast as he dared along the twisting old road back to the farm.

What did it mean — Debbie's dancing on television with Michael Thornton? His thoughts were chaotic. Seeing her on the screen so unexpectedly had stirred him to the depths of his being. Those deep expressive dark eyes — eyes which had so often looked so kindly, so — so — lovingly — had they not looked lovingly into his? He recalled her last gaze of silent reproach in the hall when he had been so brutal to her, because he was ashamed, and could not have endured her silent reproaches. Dermot turned off the engine inside the drive gate. The night was very still, a clear green sky still held folded in the west some traces of gold and rose, like wings. Good God — those eyes — Now he knew. She had looked on him with the pure, passionate love of her heart. And now he knew that he loved her. She was the reason for his being 'bound'. She it was who made

every other girl seem like dross, and
Meriel Dean, for all her allure and her
physical beauty, cheap and even con-
temptible. Subconsciously he must have
always known that he wanted one day
to marry Debbie Holden — to keep her
at the farm, and in his house — if she
would stay and if she would marry him.
Numbed and angry, he had done
nothing about it, when he realised she
had gone. It had been a blow so
stunning that the delayed shock of it
was only now beginning to make itself
felt. Was Thornton merely a dancing
partner? That was the torturing question. He drove up to the house and saw
his mother sitting at some work through
the brightly lit uncurtained windows of
the sitting room.

'Well — did you and Meriel buy the
colt?' she smilingly inquired.

'Yes. Meriel's bought the colt. Colonel Penrose has plans for making you
more sociable!'

'Oh? How nice of him.' She looked
quickly into Dermot's unusually pale

and weary looking face, longing to ask things which must not be asked. 'And Tomlin is still interested in Big Boy?'

'Very much so, indeed, I understand. Er — anything interesting on television?'

'Oh — I don't know, my dear — I never bothered with it. Mark was so troublesome — and Mrs. Frazer rang — '

'I've a hell of a lot of old form-filling to do. So — don't wait your tea-tray, Ma! I'll probably be late.'

'You look so tired, Dermot — why not wait till tomorrow?'

'Can't. I'll raid the kitchen fridge, later. Don't worry.'

In his office with the door bolted, he flicked through the telephone directory till he found the number of the hospital in Dublin to which Debbie had said she was going. Quietly he dialled the number, and waited.

'Could I speak to Nurse Holden, please?'
'Who?'

'Nurse Deborah Holden.'

'Sorry. I don't think we have a nurse of that name — '

'You must have — very recently — on your staff. Can you make sure?'

'Just hold on — I'll enquire.'

It seemed an eternity before another cool voice sounded again. It was the Assistant Matron. 'A Nurse Holden reported for duty some time — about a fortnight ago. But I regret to say she is now a patient here, herself.'

'A patient! Are you sure — Nurse Holden — you got the name?'

'That's correct. She is very ill at the moment — complications after pneumonia. Everything possible is being done for her.'

'Serious?'

'Quite serious, I'm afraid. But,' the cheerfully professional voice went on — 'she'll pull through. Young and fundamentally very healthy and strong.'

'Which ward?'

'The fever hospital. She's in the new wing.'

'Thank you, Matron. I take it she can be visited?'

'Not at present. Nurse Holden is too

ill even to see her sister, who has been here all day and must return to the country tonight.'

'Thanks. A day or two, perhaps — ?'

'We can but hope so, indeed.'

Dermot put down the receiver and glanced at his watch. Should he tell his mother now? She'd have to be told. He thought it would be wrong to keep her in ignorance, and she'd want to come with him. Maybe that was a good idea. Mrs. Ramsay could stay in the house to look after Mark —

'What's the matter, Dermot? You're ill — ' Mrs. Gregory rose, very concerned, from her chair, a few minutes later.

'Nothing the matter with me — but — Debbie's ill. I must drive up to town immediately.'

'Debbie — ill?'

'Don't worry. She'll be all right. Only — I think we'd better go and see her.'

The colour came back into the woman's face. 'Of course — at once. Oh, poor child — that's why I haven't heard from her.'

'We can stay around — at least *I'll* stay around, until I can bring her home.'

'Here — home — why, of course! Where else would she go!' The idea seemed to inspire his mother with something very like joy.

In less than an hour later both Dermot and Mrs. Gregory, having obtained every assurance from Mrs. Ramsay about Mark and her ability to look after the little fellow — were on the road to the city and the hospital.

12

'Nurse Holden', as she thought of herself, once back into hospital routine, was aware that her illness was mainly her own fault. The fact that she became so gravely ill, however, was something neither she nor anyone else could account for. But for hours on end, Debbie was oblivious of who, or where she was, or else, at times troubled by delirious nightmares.

She had reported for duty at the hospital on the morning after her television performance, although getting up on that particular morning had been an effort after a night of most unaccustomed sleeplessness. Try as she would, once she was alone, the ache of loneliness for the place she thought of as home, would not be banished, the fear of little Mark's need of her, the hurt and astonishment of Mrs. Gregory, and — here her thoughts were pulled up as though by a blank wall — did Dermot miss her? Why had he treated her so dreadfully coldly? Was he about to become engaged, or to get married at once, to Meriel Dean? She supposed it was inevitable. Such obsessive considerations never left her except during those brief sessions of dancing, which, in any case, she felt in honour bound to keep up, until Michael Thornton's former dancing partner, Judy, had recovered.

Michael, she admitted, had been wonderful to her, and the more she saw of him, danced with him, went about with him, in her free time, the more she liked and trusted him. But all these diversions, however enjoyable and stimulating, were robbing her of much needed sleep, and the sensation of near-exhaustion was never far away, either while on duty, or otherwise occupied. Had she refused to dance with Michael on television, it would have meant for him considerable loss of a financial nature, besides which it was always a disadvantage to 'drop out' when many expert people were waiting for a chance.

She could not let down Michael, however, and hoped that she could hold out until Judy was out of hospital. It was irritating to Debbie to observe that Michael was still hopeful that she might eventually go into show business with him. So irritating was this particular subject, that it was 'forbidden ground', and she refused even to discuss it.

Coming off duty, one evening, and feeling depressed beyond anything she had ever experienced before, because of the second letter from Mrs. Gregory with news of little Mark's loneliness for her, and with a note of rebuke that Debbie had not even replied to the first letter from Abbey Farm in which questions were asked concerning her suit cases and her plans. '*And not a line to congratulate us on the arrival of our picture money, and our success in getting back all that land! How could you, Debbie? Have you completely cast* us aside, now *that it seems you no longer need us?*' How was Debbie to guess that her old friend had wept bitter tears after posting that impulsive, sad-angry letter. The truth was that deep in her secret heart, she had hoped for a line from Dermot, and Dermot was not even mentioned by his mother in either of the letters. Well — now — Debbie told herself, with contempt — perhaps this would cure her of the terrible distress of false and improbable hopes. She must reply to the letter she had just received, and ask for her cases to be sent to the hospital, and the remainder of her possessions to her sister at Rockinish.

On her way to Woodbine Avenue, where she had been invited to tea with Mrs. Thornton, which invitation she occasionally accepted, those days, her thoughts were so preoccupied by the letter from Abbey Farm that she had entered the house in Woodbine Avenue, in a sort of waking dream, only to find her hostess in bed with 'flu', and

Michael struggling in the kitchen, in a hopelessly inadequate and helpless way. 'I'm in a fix! No good at the domestic side! Thank heaven for little girls!' Smilingly, Debbie took over, not only the preparation of a meal, and the cleaning up of kitchen chores, but had attended to Mrs. Thornton, and brought her up some tea and toast, which so pleased the woman's miserable condition that she was almost overcome with gratitude. 'You really are the nicest girl ever to come to this house!' declared Mrs. Thornton, revived by aspirin and strong tea. 'But you don't look very good, yourself, my dear — I've noticed you've been looking very tired this last couple of days — I only pray you won't catch this horrible bug!'

Her young friend reassured Mrs. Thornton whom she greatly liked. But although Debbie was aware that in all likelihood, she had, indeed, caught the 'bug', she kept the knowledge of her sore throat and her own headache strictly to herself, and dosed herself that night when she went back to the hospital to try to shake off the threatened attack.

Next day, however, it was clear that all her efforts were in vain. She was ordered off duty and straightway to bed, where it was discovered that she had become the victim of pneumonia.

Michael Thornton, in genuine distress of mind, called to the hospital next evening, but was not permitted to see the patient. His remorse and self-accusing were extreme, and from that evening, day and night, he had haunted the hospital, until Debbie's sister, Letty, met him in the corridor, and sympathising with him, promised that she would phone his home, herself, the moment she had any good news.

'Where are you staying, Letty? You won't mind my calling you Letty, because Debbie has so often spoken to us about you?' A sudden idea had come into his mind.

'Oh — just in that little hotel at the

station, the Phoenix. It's noisy, but I'm lucky to have got fixed up so near both the hospital and the station. I don't drive, you see, and hotels and taxis are so expensive!' Letty looked kindly at the red-headed young man. It was obvious that he was stricken with anxiety, and that for some reason, he seemed to blame himself for Debbie's illness. It was also pretty clear to Letty's sharp perception that this Michael Thornton was behaving more like a man in love with her sister, than concerned about a mere dancing partner. 'You mustn't worry so much, Mr. Thornton. She is having the very best attention — that's what I keep telling myself, you know when I get to feeling like you do now, Michael — I should say,' she amended, smiling.

'I hope so — I'm sure you are right — I'm sure Debbie must soon be all right.' He hesitated, looking up and down the long corridor where nurses and patients moved quietly up or down under a dim light, 'Do you know, I've just been thinking, my mother would love to meet you! She and Debbie have become such friends. It would give us the greatest ease of mind if you would come and stay with us?'

'Oh — I couldn't do that — But it's most kind — ' Letty was a lot more anxious about her sister than she admitted, and Michael's concern touched her, but she thought it would be too much like an imposition to accept the invitation.

'Why ever not?' the young man insisted. 'My mother has just recovered from 'flu', and she feels certain poor Debbie was suffering from the same dose, yet waited on her, and even went through a dancing performance on the same night when she must have been running a temperature. I noticed how flushed and hot she looked. It was *then* I ought to have taken her away, but I didn't dream — ' He stopped to pace the floor. 'Look — you would do us a favour, really! Do come to us. We have the phone, and we'd be together, and therefore more useful to our patient.

My mother is really so worried she'd be relieved and cheered up to have you.'

Eventually, Letty was persuaded, and in the welcome friendliness of Michael's mother found that she was much happier than brooding in the noisy loneliness of the cheap little station hotel. She could see that in the short time she had known them, Debbie had made an extraordinary impression on her new friends. It seemed that they could not do enough to help. Not for the first time, Letty was forced to acknowledge that her sister was rather an unusual girl — and that most of Debbie's attraction for people was the immense quality of loving compassion which seemed to radiate from her, as though from some source within her somewhat ordinary appearance. This was the magic of her attraction, the secret of her popularity, and Letty found herself telling Mrs. Thornton how, even as a small girl, Debbie had always been 'like that' — the sort of girl people came to, especially when they were in need, or in trouble.

'And she is gifted! I mean — she could have been, indeed, she *should* have been a ballet dancer — she would have been a famous and outstanding dancer!' Mrs. Thornton declared, enthusiastically.

Michael, finishing a quick meal in the dining room where the two women were talking, interposed, darkly — 'She *is* already a great dancer! Pop dancing like hers is as great as any form of dancing in the world.' He pushed aside his coffee and turned to an armchair. 'I do wish you could persuade her to use her gifts and earn her living by dancing instead of hospital nursing — much as we all admire that terrific profession — don't misunderstand me. But the girl — well, a girl like Debbie is one in a million.'

Letty knew that Michael was losing his heart to her sister, and she felt sad that this was so, knowing that the girl's heart was locked to all but one man, and sighed deeply when she remembered the circumstances at home, back in Rockinish, which she was convinced was the real cause of Debbie's present position.

Three anxious days had to be lived through before her friends were permitted to visit the patient. Letty was allowed a few minutes on the third day of her sojourn with the Thorntons. She was shocked by the wan appearance of the girl, whose brown eyes seemed to have sunk back into her head, but whose old cheery smile had not altogether disappeared, even though she was too weak to talk. Nevertheless, Letty was joyfully assured that her sister would pull through, and thankfully was able to look forward to returning home to Rockinish with the good news.

A day or two later, Mrs. Thornton and Michael had been admitted, and close behind them, unobserved, until they came across to Debbie's bed, two other people walked into the private ward. They were Mrs. Gregory and

Dermot, who viewed the Thorntons with surprise and unreasonable displeasure, because having been in the city staying at a nearby hotel, they believed themselves to be the first to be informed about the patient, and the first to visit her, other than her sister. It was a momentary impression, and when the Thorntons gave place to them, stepping back into the corridor for fear of crowding Debbie into any discomfort, the impression vanished, at once.

Dermot, however, was lost to every sensation but that of concern, and an overwhelming love for the girl lying there, wide-eyed and flushed by the very fact of his presence, by the wild thrill of seeing him, again. He laid a hand over hers on the cover, but could find no words to speak. Mrs. Gregory gently bent to kiss her. But almost at once, a nurse came briskly rustling into the ward, and with a degree of sternness suggested that they leave. There had been a mistake. Nurse explained, *two* visitors had been permitted, only, and for a very brief time. Four had, somehow, penetrated into the ward.

Apologies were quietly made, but Dermot slipped an envelope under the patient's pillow. Then Mrs. Gregory left her offering of fresh flowers and fruit on a trolly beside the bed. 'We'll be back in a day or two, when you are stronger, my dear Deb.' Mrs. Gregory whispered, before disappearing.

Debbie was glad to close her eyes and submit to the soothing ministrations of her kind little nurse, even though a few moments previously the same little nurse had inspired some awe into the well-meaning visitors. Dermot's envelope lay over Debbie's heart, concealed. Unopened, it was impossible for her to guess its contents. Probably a 'get-well' card. She did not try to open the envelope just then, for nurse was inclined to linger. Later, Debbie promised herself, when she was quite alone she would open Dermot's kind message. Meanwhile, he had *come*! It was almost enough for the present. His kind grey, serious eyes had looked with immense compassion and no reproof at all, into hers. The touch of his cool, firm hand had spoken, where words could not. She thought, now, she understood. Even if he had fallen in love with Meriel, he still kept a place in his heart for Debbie? On this consoling thought Debbie slept, and nurse, drawing a sunblind, quietly left the ward, closing the door firmly behind her.

Outside in the corridor, Dermot hesitated. They had followed the Thorntons towards the exit, there being no other way out of the hospital at that point. This meant that all four met, unavoidably, in the doorway to the outer compound. 'You're Thornton, aren't you? I'm sure I remember you at Colonel Penrose's house-warming party!' Dermot observed, with a sudden unaccountable sensation of reluctance to speak, at all, and a certain chilliness in his tone.

'That's so! Dermot Gregory — of course? And this is my mother — ' Michael Thornton sketched a brief introduction. Common politeness demanded this much. But the two young men were ill at ease with each other, suspicious, and even, without conscious reason, disliking each other.

The two women, however, were quite quickly at ease, and chatted pleasantly as they all strolled across the enclosed grass compound.

'Saw that programme of yours on TV,' Dermot ventured, giving the day and time of his viewing. 'Will you explain how on earth you contrived to get Debbie Holden on to that racket? Had you both been planning and scheming for ages, about it? You must have!' The tone was intended to be jocose, but the enquiry was prompted in a deadly earnest endeavour to discover something of vital importance to himself.

'Not at all. I was in a jam. My usual partner was having her appendix removed — in a hurry, and quite suddenly — and on the same evening that she arrived in town, Debbie, bless her obliging little heart, agreed to my hectic, rushed arrangements for her to take my partner's place, to help me out. The producer's a friend of mine. We pulled a few strings — and she's an outstanding dancer, otherwise, of course, it couldn't have happened.'

'Oh, I see! I understand!' Relief like a great wave drowning former unendurable doubt, silenced Dermot for the moment. But almost immediately there was a return of anxiety. Why was this red-bearded chap here, with his mother, apparently as intimate as the Gregorys themselves, and to all appearances, seeming to have a perfect right to be there — the first visitors to the sick girl — actually in the ward, too, before the correct visiting time?

There could be no explaining or answering these speculations, for it was necessary that the two women should part at the hospital entrance where the cars were parked. That evening at their hotel, a restless Dermot proposed remaining in town — 'to attend to a few matters of business, for a few days. Convenient to wait, and drive Debbie home, too, instead of coming up again.'

His mother smiled in her heart, though too wise to do so outwardly. For a young man so normally smart and quick and cautious — almost to a fault — this sort of rationalising remark struck her as being very naïve. Satisfied that the patient was out of danger, and having secured a promise from her, next morning, when Mrs. Gregory called, alone, for a few minutes, that Debbie would come 'home to Abbey Farm to convalese', Dermot's mother decided to return home where her small grandson was, she guessed, very much in need of her, and where so much heavy work had fallen on Mrs. Ramsay's willing shoulders. Mrs. Gregory noted that Debbie seemed almost obsessively determined to continue her nursing career as soon as she was well enough, but the girl had, though almost reluctantly, promised that a few days' convalesence 'doing absolutely nothing' sounded marvellous, and just what might be needed, so long as it was clearly understood that she was coming back to hospital and her job as soon as possible.

Dermot, having sent his mother off at the station, settled down to remain in town, phoning his men back at the farm and arranging for extra help, in his own absence, and Mrs. Gregory, settling back in her corner seat in the train gave herself up to some very pleasant thoughts, ignoring her magazines and newspapers. The two people she loved most in the world were, she ventured to think, at last, finding each other. She was not blind, either, to what she termed 'a healthy bit of jealousy', caused by the presence of Michael Thornton. It had taken only a very short time and some brief observation to discover how 'the wind was blowing' with that young man, and her suspicions had been further confirmed by the attitude, and indeed, by the confidence of Mrs. Thornton herself. 'My son is immensely taken with her,' the latter enthused, 'and indeed, when he first told me about his having met 'a girl called Debbie', during a visit to Dr. Kelly in the West country, who could dance better than anyone he had ever known, I began to wonder. He was more than normally interested right from the start. And,' Mrs. Thornton laughed, 'when the young lady appeared at the house, I saw what was happening — and I confess I was delighted. The girl seems to combine all the so called 'old-fashioned' virtues, with an extraordinary talent for modern — and dramatic Pop dancing? She should have been a ballet dancer, but I dare not say this before Michael!' Mrs. Thornton had chatted on, impulsively, — 'You know, I think those two are made for each other!'

Little realising the impact of her words, Mrs. Thornton had not noticed the other woman's silence nor her vaguely troubled and sometimes averted glance. Dermot's mother was not in a position to utter a word about her own suspicions nor her wishes in the matter. She could only hope that Debbie's refusal to adopt a dancing career promised some good for her own son. She gravely admitted in her mind going home in the train, that Dermot deserved to be kept in some suspense for a while, at least! He had taken Debbie far too much for granted, for far too long. He had obviously never questioned his own exclusive right to the girl's availability. But things were bound to come right now. Surely it could not be otherwise.

It was well that Mrs. Gregory had gone back when she did, thus fortified by not unreasonable wishful thinking.

13

Big Boy was back in the home stables. Debbie was 'home', every day improving in health, every day becoming more like her old cheerful self, and, despite all precautions, every day creeping back into little familiar tasks. Mark, with shining blue eyes, had become again the girl's shadow and inseparable companion.

Dermot had, deliberately, and in a manner not to be mistaken, severed every connection with Meriel Dean, written again to Harry Tomlin, declaring that, much as he had appreciated the astonishing kindness and interest of the trainer, certain circumstances made it undesirable for him, Dermot, to leave his horse any longer in Meath. To this letter there had been no reply, and every attempt made to contact the trainer by phone proved unsuccessful.

Colonel Penrose, hurt and resentful, yet philosophic, resolved to 'let sleeping dogs lie' for the moment, and disappeared for a short business sojourn, to London, which sojourn he very much disliked, but which would leave a clear field for events to work out as they would. Interference or persuasion or cajoling he had always found to be of no avail in the ordering of other people's lives. Besides, they all had a perfect right to do as they wished. The day he left Rockinish for 'business in London' was the day on which Gregory's horse arrived, unexpectedly, driven by a stable man from Meath, to Abbey Farm, without comment from Tomlin. In the inevitable travelling of country news, this fact reached the colonel on the very day it happened.

Dermot went about, abstracted and silent, and although more prosperous in his farming than he had ever been in his life, was also more unhappy. Now that the horse was back and tried, and found to be in magnificent condition

— prepared, indeed, for anything — and well prepared for the Lakeview Races — Dermot, confused by a multitude of emotions to which he had not been accustomed, then furiously regretted that his wretched relationship with Meriel had been the cause of his sending to Tomlin for Big Boy to be sent back. It seemed now, naturally, that he had made an enemy of Tomlin, for close on the return of Big Boy, came a solicitor's letter containing a stiff request for payment for the training and keeping of the animal.

Then — and more poignant than all else in making for distress — some strange impediment made it impossible for him to talk to Debbie. It seemed to him that she avoided him, and, unable to understand his own motives, he also avoided the girl whenever possible. He told himself that it was no time to approach her with his true feelings and his intention of making her mistress of the Abbey Farm — would she agree to such a proposal. 'Back to square one', ran in his mind, but worse than square one, things were happening to Debbie which had not been in evidence before. She had grown, he thought, with a sword in his heart, detached, as well as extremely attractive, even in her appearance. The new 'hair-do', the new suits and dresses, the charming new and slightly more sophisticated make-up — her lovely boyish slimness, and that accustomed air, even more evident now, of serenity, were such that he could not bear to look upon, because his mind was tense with doubt.

Every day there arrived a letter addressed in a firm manly hand, from Dublin. Always — it lay there on the hall table among the Abbey Farm post. Mrs. Gregory at breakfast was apt to remark, smilingly, with a sort of little sigh at the same time — 'Ah — Debbie's love letter! Michael Thornton, you know — he's asked her to marry him! I suppose it was inevitable. He's even willing to give up dancing professionally and go back seriously to his law studies if she will be engaged to be married to him.'

'How do you know all this?' her son demanded, almost aggressively. Debbie was not present at breakfast, Mrs. Gregory insisting on sending her a tray to her room, pointing out that convalescence was not yet quite over.

'Well — for one thing, I suspected it when I was up there while she was in hospital, and for another thing, Michael Thornton's mother told me that he was crazy about Debbie, and for an even more sure thing, Debbie herself confessed that Michael had asked her to marry him.'

Dermot, rather white about the gills, rose in furious silence to grab a pipe. It was getting on for harvesting, and he had to be out of doors most mornings, very early. That morning he stood in silence, as though paralysed, half way between the table and the door. 'Is she — going to accept him?'

'I don't — really — know, Dermot. She hasn't told me.'

'What did she say so much for, then?'

'I don't know — she and I have few secrets, now, my dear. Whoever she marries will be a lucky fellow, but she's in no hurry about marrying —. That much I can assure you. She has her mind set on nursing, for some time at least.' Feeling somewhat hypocritical — 'but all in a good cause,' — Dermot's mother hastily left the room for the fear of betraying herself.

Late that evening when a great orange-red harvest moon was slowly climbing up over the Knockadee mountains, and the corn in the Long Acre fields was golden under a silver-rose sky, Debbie sat in the chintz window seat of her old 'bed-sitter', chin in hands, gazing out over the beautiful western countryside, with its jagged mountains serene with sun-setting, and grazing sheep like boulders far up in the heights, while down below in the fertile valley, the barley and oats and wheat were ripening, and would soon be ready for the new combine harvester which

Dermot had just purchased. She was lost in thought and reluctant to switch on a bedside lamp for reading. Her heart was again stirring with the 'trouble' of restored health and vitality, and a certain rising up of her native initiative, and independence. She had been a fortnight convalescing at the farm. She had made happy, heart-warming adjustments with little Mark and with Mrs. Gregory — and even Mrs. Ramsay, and many of the neighbouring people who had 'dropped in' to see her and bid her 'welcome back'. Of all places on earth, Debbie could think of no place where she would rather be. Now, if ever, even if she must return to nursing, was the time to get back to the old companionship with Dermot. She had observed enough of him, since her return, to know that he was desperately unhappy. Was he, after all, still thinking of Meriel? Or — could it be possible that he might be unhappy about the almost tangible break — the difference in relationship between herself and him? Sometimes, when she looked up suddenly to meet his kind grey eyes bent with such intensity upon her, as though he were trying to read her very heart — she felt convinced that Dermot returned her love. But then, again, while he was always agreeable, good-humoured, and almost embarrassingly kind to her, she had seen very little of him, compared with their constant intimacy in the old days. He was, she knew, grappling with new responsibility, new people, new workers and plans, and she allowed for all this. Yet, there was a difference. She wondered, pensively, that lovely harvest-like evening, if it were possible ever to pick up the broken pieces of a friendship and put them together again, when once the lovely mould was broken? Looking into her heart, numbed and resigned since her illness, but now beginning to stir with the old agony of loving Dermot, she faced the fact that she could not marry Michael Thornton — ever. Even if she were to lose sight of Dermot — even if, despite all that had happened, Dermot might one day, yet, marry Meriel Dean, *she* could not marry Michael. She had too great a regard, too much of a sort of loving in another way — to bring to him a heart in marriage full of passionate love for another man.

Next morning, after breakfast, Debbie strolled out-of-doors — over to the near paddock, to see Big Boy, who was just then playfully galloping round the fence, his fine head held high, and his mane flying in a lively breeze. She called to him as she leaned over the gate, and he remembered her and came trotting towards her to be rewarded with the usual tit-bit. He was in wonderful form, his coat gleaming, every magnificent muscle vibrant with life and energy. She talked to him, caressing his velvet nose, until Dermot, whom she had believed to be miles away on business, that morning, emerged from the nearby stables.

Her heart racing, she called out, to

cover her surprise and embarrassment,
— 'Dermot, he wants to talk to you! Er
— he is in a gossipy sort of mood
— time he was back in his stable, isn't
it?'

The young man stopped short in his
walk across the yard, surprised, too, at
Debbie's being about so early. He
dropped some harness on to the
cobbles and came at once across to the
gate to stand beside her. 'High time
— if he were seriously training!'

She turned round. 'Oh, why did you
withdraw him from Meath, and from
the Lakeview races? It was criminal of
you!' For the moment, she had really
forgotten everything else but the horse,
and the pity of his not running at
Lakeview.

'I had my reasons,' Dermot replied,
curtly. 'I had no alternative.'

'Yes.' She turned away her face. 'I
know. Your mother told me — about
you and Meriel. But surely, whatever
happened between you and Meriel, you
need not have done anything quite so

extreme? So uncalled for? Looks like revenge, or — or bad temper, or even fear!'

His grey glance met hers, steadily. 'I once told you that Meriel Dean meant nothing to me. And for your further information, I had no choice. The animal arrived back here. I wasn't consulted. But — ' he stepped back a little from where he had been leaning beside her over the gate, 'you don't understand. How could you understand, anyway. I've paid Tomlin for his interest and his services. I am under no compliment to him. Big Boy will run in other races.' He straightened up, about to go away.

Debbie found herself asking, with a sort of compulsive urgency — 'Dermot — why are you so *different* — so horrid, even, sometimes, nowadays? We used to be such friends.' Reproachfully, she gazed at the thin, weather-beaten face, the new hard lines about the mouth, the sad grey eyes she so adored, now growing angry, even as they met and compelled her own.

'*You* should know why! You will soon be off and away with your red-bearded dancer! So — nothing here can possibly matter very much to *you*, any more.' He spoke with a bitterness she had never heard in his voice before.

'That's not true! I'm as interested and concerned and involved as ever, about Abbey Farm, and — '

But it was too late to explain further. Dermot had turned on his heel and was off across the yard to pick up his harness, and disappear.

For a few wild moments she thought of following him — of running to put her arms tight about his neck. He was jealous! *Now* she saw, plainly, as she had not seen before — Dermot was jealous of Michael Thornton, so he must love her? Dermot must love her! She stood for a few ecstatic moments leaning over the gate, again caressing the nose of the horse before 'shooing' him off on a mock-frightened canter away up the field. A wild delight ran in the girl's veins. Her happiness was suddenly almost unbearable — Dermot must surely love her! Every puzzling memory fitted into place. *Now*, she understood. She was safe. Her ship of life had sailed into the haven where she would be. There was work to be done — things to be faced, maybe a little storm or two — lots of humiliation, perhaps, on her part — but these were only small hurdles to be crossed.

How long she remained, leaning over the gate with the mellow gold of the sunny morning on her face, and the breeze in her hair, she never knew, until she was disturbed out of her waking dream by the sound of Mrs. Ramsay's footsteps hurrying down the yard. 'Oh, Miss Debbie, the colonel on the phone — '

'He can't be, Mrs. Ramsay — he's in London.'

'He's back. Flew over last night, and Mr. Tomlin is with him, over in Penrose House, this minnit! They want Mr. Dermot at once — '

'Oh, well, he was here talking to me only a little while ago. At least, not very long ago — ' Debbie glanced quickly into the nearby stables and outhouses. She saw Mike crossing the yard and shouted her question across to him — 'Is Mr. Dermot about, Mike?'

'Gone off on his old bike, Miss — 'gone fishin'', he said — true as I'm standin' here, Miss!' Mike shook his head — 'Shouldn't wonder if Mr. Gregory is sicknin' for somethin', Miss? 'Gone fishin'' — did ye' ever hear the like.'

'He was probably joking, Mike, but he's wanted on the phone — '

'He wasn't jokin', Miss. He took his tackle with him.'

Debbie ran back into the house, with Mrs. Ramsay sailing somewhat sedately, and disapprovingly, in her wake. Mrs. Gregory had just put down the receiver, and was looking annoyed. 'Isn't it maddening — Dermot having disappeared so mysteriously — what can he be thinking of? He must have known

Colonel Penrose had come home and wanted to speak to him — Dermot wanted to avoid a *tete-à-tête*! That's it, obviously, a disgusting sort of thing to do.'

'I don't think he had a clue about the colonel being back, Mrs. Gregory. Why — I was talking to Dermot only a little while ago, and you know, as well as I do he would *never* do a thing like that!' Debbie was pink with indignation at the suggestion, pleasing the young man's mother in a way she had no conception of, at that moment.

'Well — no, he wouldn't. That's true, dear,' Mrs. Gregory agreed, soothingly. 'But it's so awkward — you see, Mr. Tomlin wants to speak to him, *urgently*, and I bet it's about Big Boy.'

'It could be, I suppose. But there's just nothing we can do, at the moment. I expect Dermot will appear any moment. He's probably gone down to Kellys' to enquire after John's wife and new baby! He's always pulling Mike's leg. Did you want me to go into

Rockinish for the the meat?' She changed the subject, quickly.

'Oh, yes — yes — They've forgotten to send it, and Mrs. Ramsay is waiting on it.' Mrs. Gregory paused. 'I don't know if I should even mention this, as Dermot isn't here, but I *can*, to *you*, dear Deb. And I simply *must* tell you that Tomlin says there has been some misunderstanding. He says he never sent Dermot that bill, and that Meriel is the cause of all the trouble — Poor Colonel Penrose is most upset. He keeps trying to cover up for Meriel, of course, but I fear she's been up to no good, and Tomlin wants to have Big Boy run at Lakeview! Just think — wouldn't it be wonderful!'

Stunned a little, Debbie stood wide-eyed, trying to adjust to what she had been told. 'It would be the most wonderful thing ever happened,' she breathed, excitement shining in her brown eyes. 'But I'd better go for the meat, or we'll have no lunch! Come

Markie. We're going shopping, and as it's a bit windy, I'll buy you those balloons I promised you.'

'Oh, Goody! Oh, I'm glad Debbie's home, Nana!' Mark jumped up and down several times, and ended by rolling on the carpet to express his delight.

'Silly boy! Come on, then. We're in a hurry.'

Later, putting the meat into the boot of the little car, with some other purchases for the kitchen, Debbie was about to step into the driver's seat, when the 'clip-clop' of horses' shoes on the cobbled street, attracted her attention, and looking round, she saw Meriel Dean leading her own hunter Noble, round towards the stables beside Penrose House. The two girls met face to face, and buoyed up by some inner confidence and secret happiness, Debbie was the first to speak, and to speak with a friendly note in her voice.

'You're horse is coughing — I do hope nothing's wrong — ?'

'I've just been to the vet. Noble is out — for Lakeview.' Meriel announced, abruptly. 'He's coughing badly.' Meriel's beautiful blue eyes were blazing with anger, and brilliant unshed tears.

'Oh, Meriel — I'm sorry. I really am terribly sorry.' The younger girl patted the animal's neck, impulsively. 'What a rotten shame — on the very eve of the races.'

'It's not usual with you to be hypocritical, Nurse Holden!' Meriel snapped. 'Why should *you* be sorry! Anyhow, they're all making such a fuss and blaming *me*, too, about Big Boy — *He'll* run at Lakeview I'm told now, so all's rose-coloured for you, up there at the farm!'

Colonel Penrose appeared at the hall door, having seen the girls from a window inside.

Debbie hesitated, but in a flash her mind was made up. She ran up the steps while Meriel took her horse round to the stable. 'I've just heard the news from Meriel. Oh, — it's too bad! And

Noble was in such form! To get a cough on the eve of the races — I'm so very sorry, Colonel Penrose.'

'It's a damnable disappointment. Do come in. I'm all thumbs, and my percolator has gone wrong — ' He went before her into the dining room, where a coffee percolator was bubbling over on to the table. 'Shocking business — the whole thing — apart from Noble. Can you fix this yoke, Debbie?'

She smiled at the colonel's lapse into colloquial usage, as she quickly put the percolator to rights and mopped the table. Then she filled out a cup of coffee for her host, and on being pressed to do so, filled a cup for herself and Meriel, who was just then, coming into the room.

Meriel accepted the coffee, ungraciously, in silence, then moved to the window, turning her back on the other two. Her father looked wretched, and when he had swallowed his coffee, he excused himself, and left the room.

'Mrs. Dean — er — Meriel — please

— I do want to speak to you,' the other girl said, urgently.

Meriel swung round. 'Since you force me to it — *I* don't want to talk to *you*! I wish you'd go! The Gregorys — and it looks like you're almost one of them, now — have made it quite plain they don't intend any further intimacy with us. So, why are *you* here?'

'Because your father was nice enough to ask me to come in.'

'Well, say on! Are you going to tell me the date of your marriage to Dermot Gregory! You schemed that well! However, none of my business now.'

Debbie reddened, but stood her ground. 'You are upset, so I won't allow those unkind words to affect me. If Noble is out of the running, why not let Dermot's horse take his place — I mean, why not run Big Boy as coming from your own stables and Mr. Tomlin's? Only for you, Harry Tomlin would never have heard of Dermot's horse. So it would be nothing but the truth, Big Boy is your own achievement, and you have a perfect right? Couldn't something like that be done?'

Meriel had been staring at her unwelcome caller more and more wide-eyed with amazement, until a small contemptuous smile dawned on her face. 'I didn't think you were quite so ignorant as all that, Nurse Holden! Imagine living up there at Abbey Farm for five or six years — with a family whose interest in horses goes back generations — and be so damned green.'

'Why — '

'Before setting out on any project, you should at least know a few facts about it!'

'I — I don't understand,' Debbie floundered, getting more and more painfully scarlet cheeked.

'Of course you don't understand. That's why you should keep off this particular grass. You are just being silly — what do you know about horse-racing!'

Debbie drew herself up. Her colour had changed. Anger and embarrassment had made her as white as she had been red a few minutes previously. Her dark eyes smouldered. 'I suppose I am an outsider about such technicalities! Admitted! But, since I truly wanted to be helpful. I don't see why you should be so — nasty!'

'Nasty!' Meriel laughed a harsh little laugh. 'I'm just made that way, I suppose. Anyway, I don't suffer fools gladly.'

'Well, explain, please. Since you've gone so far in plain speaking!'

'You couldn't possibly substitute a horse for another in a race!'

'Oh — no — I suppose not.' Debbie sat down looking at the toes of her shoes. 'No, you couldn't do that. I see.' She knew Meriel was looking at her with amused contempt. But, bracing herself, she went on — 'I thought Big Boy had been duly signed up, you know — in the official form sent by the Horse Breeder's Society, when he was a foal, with a vet to verify, and all that.'

'Naturally. Dermot saw to all that. It goes without saying. But for entering the horse in a race at Lakeview, he'd have to be registered there ages ago — his pedigree, his achievements. Dermot's horse has thoroughbred blood on his sire's side, but a little less than that out of the mare. Harry Tomlin has all those details.'

'But — presumably, since Mr. Tomlin has been training and feeding and running Big Boy at various functions over there with all sorts of horses, in Meath, he must believe in him — and he said he could have him fit for Lakeview because Dermot had been working with the animal in his spare time for months — he must have entered him with Dermot's co-operation, for Lakeview.'

Meriel went to the cocktail cabinet and poured out a whiskey for herself, offering nothing to Debbie, every look and movement of her behaviour being prompted by jealousy and even hatred of the other girl, and deliberately intended to be insulting. She made no answer to Debbie's last observation. But at that moment men's voices sounded in the hall, and Colonel Penrose with Harry Tomlin entered the room.

'Debbie — I think you know our friend Tomlin — the finest trainer in the country!' Meriel's father introduced them as though no emotional storm were evident in his daughter's flushed countenance.

Harry Tomlin threw his tweed hat, carelessly, on a chair, and sat down, very much at his ease, and quite coolly, beside Meriel who had taken her whiskey to the settee. 'Ah, Miss Holden — heard about you, I think. Can you explain where the devil Gregory has disappeared to? I've been trying to get him on the 'phone all morning. There's been a mistake — er — a stupid mistake on Johnston's, my secretary's part, while I was in France. Only just heard about it. That horse has been entered for Lakeview — and what's more — that horse is going to run at Lakeview! But where the hell is Dermot Gregory? Because we have to put things straight for him at once. I've come up from my stables for no other reason, this morning, and I have to get back as soon as possible.'

'It wasn't Johnston's fault — or mistake — whatever you like to term it — And well you know it!' Meriel flashed.

'That's not the point now! So long as we can put it right before it's too late. Gregory is an obstinate type of a fellow.' The thin brown-skinned man smiled wryly at Meriel, putting an iron-firm hand on her shoulder. 'We can put the whole matter straight, now, if we set about it, and then we can forget it — eh?' It was obvious that there was more implied meaning than the words' literal utterance indicated.

'It's no concern of mine, any more. I'm giving up the idea of a riding school here — I'm going back to England.' She freed herself from Tomlin's hand and went to the cabinet where her father had a drink ready for him. Meriel took the glass and crossed the room, handing it to the trainer. 'I don't care now who knows it — she'll hear about it, anyway,' Meriel indicated Debbie. 'Bound to hear all about it, because Johnston has resigned on the head of it and he'll spread it about the country-side — with additions of his own, no doubt! While you were in France, I persuaded Johnston to send back Dermot Gregory's horse! I lied and cheated and got the bill sent. The plan didn't come off because you came home before you were expected — that's all there's to it. I'm out of it, now, and you can all do as you like about Lakeview. I won't be there, anyway.'

'Oh, I think you will, Meriel!' Harry sampled his drink and urged Meriel down on to the settee beside him. 'And it's just rot about your going away from home again and giving up the idea of the riding school — your father's been telling me all this nonsense.'

'Meriel's never done a thing like this in her life,' Colonel Penrose interposed, quickly. 'She thought Dermot really meant it when he suggested, as he did suggest, that he should have his horse back.'

'Well, *that's* something he just *couldn't do*!' Tomlin laughed a little grimly. 'The fellow was drunk when he said that. I took no heed of it, of course.'

Meriel dabbed her eyes, making no secret of the fact that she was then crying, bitterly.

'Too bad about Noble. Rotten luck! Come — shed those tears here!' Tomlin offered his shoulder, and to Debbie's, and, indeed, the colonel's delighted surprise, the blonde head was laid with a certain reluctant relief on the proffered shoulder. It was clear that the wiry, thin, wise man was intending to devote the rest of his life in an endeavour to 'tame', and if necessary, to control the reins of life for Meriel Dean.

Debbie jumped up. 'Listen — I have an idea where Dermot is! I'll go at once — I'm almost certain I'm right. The moment he knows you are here, Mr. Tomlin, he'll come right up to you here — to Penrose House.'

14

Debbie rushed into the kitchen at the farm, to find Mrs. Ramsay, very disgruntled, opening a tin of meat, and in process of changing the luncheon menu. 'I've just had to put back the whole thing till tomorrow! What on earth kept you? You'll just have to put up with pot-luck, today. I'm not a magician! Can't produce food for the dining room when there's none brought in from the shops!'

'Whatever you give us is always delicious, Mrs Ramsay, honestly! Don't worry about it. We shall enjoy it tomorrow. I was delayed — unavoidably — but I'm so sorry to be late.'

'I'm not blaming you, Miss — but — '

'I am blameworthy!' Debbie laughed. 'But I'm sure I'd have your sympathy and maybe your support, if you knew what delayed me! And, I say, Mrs. Ramsay, let's have honey crumpets for sweet! I'll get the mixer going.' She took down a big yellow bowl from the shelf, and found the electric mixer. 'Mrs. Gregory likes them as much as I do — and Dermot adores them! I mean — he'd devour the entire dish-full, if you didn't watch!'

'Yes, but he won't be here for lunch! Isn't he 'gone fishin'' — Did you ever! I thought Mike was pullin' my leg, but no, it appears Master Dermot took the gear with him, and went off on the old bike. Moped in here for some biscuits an' stuffed them in a pocket an' said somethin' about not bein' home till night, an' not to wait any meals for him.'

'Goodness! Does Mrs. Gregory know?'

'Couldn't say. She's shut up there in the sitting room with a crowd o' ladies from Rockinish — wanti' her to go on some committee, or other. 'Course everybody wants the Gregorys to go on some committee or other, nowadays!'

Mrs. Ramsay sniffed. 'Signs on it — we're all socially goin' up in the world!'

'Now then, Mrs. Ramsay — not to be cynical! And you're probably quite wrong. It's only that Mrs. Gregory is no longer an invalid.' Debbie was changing into old jeans and high boots. She had glanced at the clock and made a quick decision. 'Look, Mrs. Ramsay — can you see to Mark's dinner? I'm sorry to have to say we can't have crumpets, because *I* won't be here, either if Dermot is not to be here for the meal. I've something to do, and must fly. Tell you all about it, some day!'

'I can see somethin's brewin'! O.K., Miss. I'll have a packed lunch ready for two by the time you have this young man's kite and those balloons you bought him, sky-high!'

'Bless you, Mrs. Ramsay.' Debbie took the child out on the lawn, and soon the brightly coloured balls and the kite were floating upwards into an airy blue and white sky, while the boy

319

shouted with delight, and Debbie herself, in some mysterious sort of kinship, felt her spirits rise and float away into a world of light-hearted content. The lattice windows of the sitting room were open, and several interested ladies looked out to cheer and wave to them, while Debbie found an opportunity to explain things to Mrs. Gregory.

Then, once more, the girl was off towards the mountains and the glen, and in less than half an hour she had come to a wild upland cross-roads where the car must be left. Taking the picnic basket with her, she started the rough walk down Knockadee Glen, the Owenbeg river running parallel on one side, horned sheep crossing the path from time to time. The mountains rose in purples of ling and early heather, and the gold of bracken shining in the breezy uplands, making a lovely contrast to the greens of pine trees, dark or light, which crowded the lower slopes. It was a walk, familiar and loved, which always brought happiness to Debbie. The day continued breezy, but the sun's heat was increasing. The girl thought, again, whimsically, as she had thought, seeing Mark's balloons sailing, that it was a day made for happiness, enhanced now by the gentle, continuous cooing of doves from the depths of the pine forest below in the far glen. The river tumbled in blue flashes, and once she stopped to look down, remembering, into a pool where the waters were smooth and clear and ultramarine, and where shallow streamlets falling from the heights, tumbled, silver and amber, at her feet. Here, she and Dermot, had, in times past, when she had first come to the Abbey Farm, sat and talked and been happy, as new friends often are on the exciting borders of discovering each other.

But now, if Dermot really had come away 'fishin'', it was hereabouts she must certainly find him.

And was not mistaken. In the

distance, round a curve of the Knock-adee mountain, where the water had again widened, between bulrushes and rough grasses, she saw a man's figure out in waders, throwing his line. It was Dermot. She was sure of it when she came nearer, walking very quickly by then, and intent only on what lay before her.

He did not see her until she stopped almost opposite him on the shingly bank where the pebbles beneath her feet were as white as marbles and polished to a satin smoothness by the continuous rush of waters meeting above them. Then, looking up, he stared, intently, for a few moments, his face as far as she could distinguish in the distance, quite devoid of expression.

'Hi! Hi, there! Dermot!' she called out, scattering horned sheep, who took to the shallow water on their way to an island in the middle of the still pool. 'Don't pretend you neither see nor hear me — because you do!' She laughed. 'Come and share some nice lunch!

Better than a few old dry biscuits.'

For some moments there was no answer, because the young man seemed concentrating on his line. But without lifting his head he called out — 'Discovering the way to a fellow's heart, eh? Through his belly! No peace left anywhere from you, women! What brings you here, anyway?'

'Come on — I want to talk to you, when you finish off that fellow. I hate to see him flapping, poor devil.' She shouted, seeing that he really had landed a fish, and was unhooking it from its hook. 'And despite your rudeness, you see, I've brought you luck! I'll bet you haven't had a catch till I came along!'

She found a place among the dry grass and stones, to sit, with the picnic basket beside her, and her brown hands folded between her knees, waiting. Amused, she watched his deliberately unhurried movements, the fixing of his gear, his somewhat ostentatious glances at the sky, and up the river. It wasn't going to be easy to talk him round to his normal 'niceness' and common sense. She could see that at a glance. But to hurry would be fatal. Harry Tomlin would just have to wait. She was about to confront someone more important, to herself, than anyone else in the world, and for once, she was going to consider her own happiness and that of Dermot, before anyone or anything. With a quiet confidence, she sat and waited. He left his gear in a rock-shaded place, and with even, smooth, strides, moved out from the wide waters into the rushing shallows. In a few minutes he was there, standing beside her, opening the the creaking lid of a fishing basket to display his catch. He had several trout besides the last one, lying in the basket. He passed no remark, but went over to a cool shady spot to leave the basket.

'I see! O.K.! I take it all back — congratulations!'

'Still, there's no saying but that you might bring me luck, yet — all the same,' he admitted, pulling off the waders, and drawing some dry socks and sandals from a pocket.

She produced two flasks of coffee and two plastic boxes of very good food. 'Now — a large mug, and even brown sugar if you want it, for the coffee, and sit down and relax.'

'Why are you here? How did you know I was here? And — what the devil are you following me round for? What can you possibly have to say to *me* in your present circumstances?'

'Lots!'

'Indeed?' He looked at her enquiringly. 'Well, let's have it, so, Nurse Debbie.' He swallowed some coffee and flung a pebble into the stream.

Debbie bit into a ham sandwich and chewed it in silence for a few moments, completely 'at sea' as to the wisest point at which to begin what she had to say.

'Well — Talk! Thornton, I suppose? That daft pop-dancer made of india rubber, with the red beard!'

His companion handed him some

ham rolls when she did begin to talk — and not in the least in the manner she had intended. 'Michael Thornton is my friend — and I'll thank you to keep your tongue in order when you mention him. I'll bet he can do things with his legs and feet you can't do, anyway!'

'No doubt! But you've hardly come off here into Knockadee Glen just to discuss Thornton's legs? Or have you?' He gave her a long sideways glance. 'You know, Debbie Holden I used to think — ' he stopped for a moment or two — 'well, no matter now what I *used* to think about you, and the qualities you had in you, and the character you had that a man could sort of — well — sort of depend his life on! Now I perceive you are just like any other bit of a 'teenage popster'!'

Brushing some crumbs from her jeans, she made as if to rise. But he stretched out a quick hand to detain her. 'Don't go! We'll say you're a mixed bag — like the rest of us.'

'All right. I'll stay. But you'd better be civil!'

'Right. I'll be civil.' He found a wheaten bread roll, placed a piece of ham on it and began to eat it with some appreciation. 'When is it coming off, anyway, the wedding, I mean?' He stared away towards the top of Knockadee floating in a maze of blue and white and gold.

'What wedding?'

'Yours, naturally — to Thornton?'

'Who told you I was going to marry Michael Thornton?'

'Well — for one — my own mother told me — at least she told me you had got yourself engaged to him. So — I added the little sum together and it seemed to make logic. Pardon the mixed metaphors!'

'Your arithmetic and your logic are out — dead out, for once! I'm not marrying Michael, nor was I, actually ever engaged to him, although he asked me to be engaged to him and to marry him — and for a little while, I thought, maybe I would. I like him — very, very much.' She watched Dermot's averted profile still staring at the mountain top. 'The trouble is that I don't just happen to think of him in that light. That's all! I mean, I'd want to be in love with the man I intended to marry.'

Dermot's face was very red when he turned towards her. Then he put down his coffee mug, pushed the box of food on one side, and moved up to sit close beside her. Debbie continued eating her lunch, although it was threatening to choke her, so madly was her heart beating. His ardent grey eyes were earnestly seeking her own, his hand under her chin, forcing her to look at him.

'Debbie — talk to me — what's in your heart — what's in your mind — my dear love?' He took the cup of coffee out of her hand and drew her into his arms. 'Why have we been so estranged? Why did you go away? Why — why — oh, why have you almost driven me mad, and broken my heart

— thinking you were going to tie up with Thornton, and leave us, for good?'

She hid her face in his shoulder, making no protest at being held in a sudden vice-like grip, within his arms. 'I had been so long — so very long loving you, Dermot — hopelessly — for who was *I* to love *you*? I believed you were intending to marry Meriel. I thought you were — just being chivalrous — to me.'

'Good God! But didn't you know, long since, that I'm the least chivalrous man on earth! How could you accuse me of such a thing! No — because now that we're beginning to talk sense, I can tell you I wouldn't have *let* you marry Thornton! Stay right here! This is where you belong! In my arms!'

Debbie stayed, and ceased struggling, partly because she desperately wanted to stay, and partly because she had no alternative.

'No, I was intending to *make* you love me, to hold on to you, to keep you at the Abbey Farm — if I had to lock you up there! And in the final effort, I was going to use Mark, ruthlessly and with malice aforethought — I knew, if Mark couldn't 'take it', you wouldn't leave us — at least not for ages, by which time I had it all fixed that you'd be in a mood to marry me!' His hard, passionate kiss was on her mouth for the first time. Debbie's warm arms tightened about his neck, and for some considerable time, the stream's babbling and the cooing doves and the sighing pines had all the golden silence of the afternoon to themselves.

Aeons later, it seemed Debbie managed to escape a whirlwind onslaught of loving — a realm of immensity — a sense of near-drowning in some hitherto unplumbed depths. She jumped up to her feet, running down to the edge of the chattering golden streamlet, to bathe her burning cheeks, to laugh, to call Dermot to come for a quick swim, 'before they said another word' — 'Because — listen, my darling,' she laughed, 'I have yet more to say to you

— and I can't imagine how you are going to take it!'

'Swim? In my skin, or my pants?' he demanded, with a great show of seriousness.

'Whichever you like!' She laughed merrily. 'I pushed in my old togs in the basket — don't know why — and I'm going off down the bend into a rock pool away from your old trout! Be seeing you!'

Before the young man could quite collect his scattered thoughts and impressions, Debbie was flying off down the glen, turning once, to wave, before disappearing beyond a bank of jutting rocks.

Later, there was more hot coffee, and more talking in the sheltered nook. 'You see, Dermot, there was something else I felt I *had* to do — to face up to — something I felt I simply must *do* something about. That's what I thought at the time, but I wonder — was it outrageous cheek on my part — and will you ever forgive me? That's what

I'm afraid of, now.'

'Here she goes again!' With mock resignation, Dermot settled his head in Debbie's lap, closing his eyes against the sun, imprisoning her hands against his face. 'Dear, quixotic, unpredictable Deb! Out with it!'

'I — I've made arrangements — of course you can still cancel them — ' she hurried on. 'Actually, I've made arrangements for Big Boy to run at Lakeview!' She waited to draw away her hands, but they were still tightly imprisoned, and she drew a long secret breath of relief. Beyond the involuntary gripping of her hands, however, there was no other response for a little while, beyond a quiet laugh. Then Dermot sat up, hugging his knees.

'Queer — I came away 'fishing' today, not really to fish, in the first instance. That was only incidental. Though, mind you. I've discovered fishing's a great way to clear a man's mind of cobwebs and help him to decisions. I had made up my mind before I was half an hour down in the pool there. I knew what I had to do. I couldn't get it out of my head — the way you were looking at that horse this morning. I couldn't help agreeing with every word you said, about it being a disgrace to keep the animal back from the races. I felt a heel when I walked away from you. No matter what Tomlin has done since. I was intending coming back home to phone him, myself — to *ask* him to let my horse run, after all! Just about the time I hooked that last trout! Then I looked up and saw you here — and somehow it seemed as if it were a sort of sign from heaven or something — that I had made a right decision.'

'And you never mentioned it to me!' she accused, in turn.

'No — well, I just wanted to hear what you had to say, first. That's my way, I'm afraid. I have to be dead sure of a thing — ' He laughed suddenly, pulling Debbie down beside him. 'Now then, Mrs. Dermot Gregory-to-be, please God, what do you think of *that* for two minds with but a single thought! What do you think of *that* for seeing 'eye-to-eye', and conjugal agreement!'

'Oh, I think it's wonderful — ' whispered Debbie, almost faint with the ecstasy of lying there in the sweet purple ling and heather in his arms. But she sat up again, and brushing back her silky brown fringe, she said, quickly — 'I ought to have told you before this, Meriel's horse is sick — he's coughing. He can't run at Lakeview! You can imagine the blow to her and to Colonel Penrose. So — you see, *that's* why I suddenly found myself making the most ridiculous suggestions. It's idiotic for anyone to suggest things out of one's own sphere. I meant well — but was just laughed at, naturally. I offered Big Boy in Noble's place — to run as her own. I deserved to be smiled at, Dermot — only I do wish she didn't dislike me so much — I do wish she had understood — that I meant to be helpful.'

Dermot took her arm. 'We'd better get back — Don't worry about Meriel. She'll come round — and if not — that's her loss, my love, not yours.'

'Yes, but there's even more,' Debbie panted standing straight in front of him. 'But this is the *nice* part of it!' In a few brief sentences she had explained Meriel's confession, Tomlin's presence at Rockinish, with the colonel, and the fact that the trainer was there for no other purpose than to talk to Dermot, whom he had been trying to contact all day.

'And *you* only tell me this now!' roared Dermot. But it was a shout of sheer joy. 'Now — what? I know — we'll leave the old bike and the fish here, till tonight or sometime, I'll send one of the lads for them. Where's your car?'

'At the glen head, of course.'

'We'd better get there, and to Penrose House, as fast as your little old mouse-trap can take us!' He took Debbie's hand, and they ran, Debbie laughingly protesting at her mini-Austin being so termed, but having to give up the attempt for want of breath.

In the car, Dermot was thoughtful, till they came in sight of the town. 'We'll make him our wedding present to them — to Tomlin and Meriel!'

'What!' his companion almost gasped. 'You mean you'll actually *give* them your horse? Oh, no!'

'Why not!' Dermot laid a quick hand on Debbie's knee. 'Kings have been known to part with thrones — I'm glad to part with a horse in order to — maybe to please something in myself. Big Boy is a worthy gift to a man I think a lot of — to a man I admire and respect — Tomlin!' He paused before amending, 'as for Meriel — ' He grinned, 'Well, we must admit she has taken a great interest in him. In a way, he's been bound up with her for weeks — months — past. Let's give them Big Boy, and be done with it.

Eh, Deb? He belongs to the past, as far as we are concerned.'

'I see what you mean. I agree. In fact — I'm glad, Dermot! And we can buy another horse, can't we?'

'We can, and we will — the best Tomlin's stables can offer. He will be yours and mine, Debbie. Our very own horse.'

'Oh, yes — Dermot — *ours*!'

'Besides which, my girl, you'll have to begin to learn a bit of stable language, and racing, and the ways of horses! You're a preposterously ignorant child about such things! And now you're to be a Gregory — '

'Oh I shall have to get cracking at my horsey alphabet! Ah, well, I'm learning! I say — there's your mother and poor little Markie waiting for us!'

'Get out, Deb.' He held open the door. 'I'll go along up right away just as I am, to meet Tomlin. You fix up things in there? Tell Ma the news!' He kissed her flushed, happy cheek and waved to his mother. 'You'll be at home in there when I come back — in an hour or so — we'll have to have a little celebration — even if it's only the usual tea-tray!'

'Yes, I'll be waiting for you, darling Dermot — at home!'

We do hope that you have enjoyed reading this large print book.

Did you know that all of our titles are available for purchase?

We publish a wide range of high quality large print books including:
Romances, Mysteries, Classics
General Fiction
Non Fiction and Westerns

Special interest titles available in large print are:
The Little Oxford Dictionary
Music Book, Song Book
Hymn Book, Service Book

Also available from us courtesy of Oxford University Press:
Young Readers' Dictionary
(large print edition)
Young Readers' Thesaurus
(large print edition)

For further information or a free brochure, please contact us at:
Ulverscroft Large Print Books Ltd.,
The Green, Bradgate Road, Anstey,
Leicester, LE7 7FU, England.
Tel: (00 44) **0116 236 4325**
Fax: (00 44) **0116 234 0205**

LOVE WILL FIND A WAY

Joan Reeves

Texan Darcy Benton would give anything to be the kind of woman who could captivate her new boss Chase Whitaker. However, the sexy CEO would hardly fall for someone like Darcy, with her straight-laced office wardrobe. Enter Darcy's matchmaking pal, Janet. She transforms her into a bombshell worthy of Chase's undying devotion. Darcy is soon letting her hair down and swapping her boxy suits for slinky dresses. And as Chase becomes intrigued — he's ready for anything . . . including true love.

PICTURES OF THE PAST

Jean M. Long

Lydia's Aunt Mattie goes on a cruise with her friend Joel, and asks Lydia to run her guesthouse near Ullswater. But Joel's nephew Luke Carstairs is also there to help, and Lydia resents his interference. She also resents his interest in her family history, and his reticence to talk about his own background. And what is the mystery about the old photograph album? How can Lydia find the truth, and cope with her growing attraction to Luke?

NANNY WANTED

Noelene Jenkinson

Melbourne businesswoman, Elly George, has her life planned out. But then she employs Environmental Engineer and part-time nanny, Rusty Webster, to care for her eight-month-old god-child Molly. Living close together in her apartment, attraction and romance blossom. However, whilst Elly is an only child and career woman, Rusty comes from a large family and wants one of his own. Elly keeps her distance, believing that they are not suited. But is her career going to be enough for Elly?

REMEMBER YESTERDAY

Kate Cartwright

Elaine Barrington's mother-in-law resents the fact that she survived the car crash that killed Michael, Elaine's husband, and left her teenaged daughter Deborah with a limp. And Deborah blames her mother for the 'careless moment', which ruined her life. Added to that, there is jealousy when mother and daughter are attracted to the same man, Andrew Nicholson. It's only when Elaine disappears that the strain she has endured is realised, and Andrew convinces Rachel and Deborah of the truth.

WHISPERS FROM THE PAST

Sheila Benton

A letter from the past reveals a shocking secret that rocks Francine's world. Her place in life and everything secure and substantial crumble away. In a desperate attempt to find where she belongs, she travels to another country and tries to build a new life. Gradually the pieces fall into place and the shadows disappear. But the past pulls her back as she decides between not just two countries — but two men . . .